Perils and Lace

A Ghostly Fashionista Mystery

Gayle Leeson

Grace Abraham Publishing

Gayle Leeson
Grace Abraham Publishing
A Division of Washington Cooper, Inc.
13335 Holbrook St.
Bristol, Virginia 24202

Publisher's Note: This is a work of fiction. Names, characters, places, and incidents are a product of the author's imagination. Locales and public names are sometimes used for atmospheric purposes. Any resemblance to actual people, living or dead, or to businesses, companies, events, institutions, or locales is completely coincidental.

Book Layout ©2017 BookDesignTemplates.com

Ordering Information:
Quantity sales. Special discounts are available on quantity purchases by corporations, associations, and others. For details, contact the "Special Sales Department" at the address above.

Perils and Lace/ Gayle Leeson -- 1st ed.
ISBN 978-1-7320195-1-5

Also by Gayle Leeson

A Ghostly Fashionista Mystery Series

Designs on Murder
Perils and Lace

Down South Café Mystery Series

The Calamity Café
Silence of the Jams
Honey-Baked Homicide
Apples and Alibis

Kinsey Falls Chick-Lit Series

Hightail It to Kinsey Falls
Putting Down Roots in Kinsey Falls
Sleighing It in Kinsey Falls

Victoria Square Series (With Lorraine Bartlett)

Yule Be Dead
Murder Ink

A Murderous Misconception

Writing as Amanda Lee

Embroidery Mystery Series

The Quick and the Thread
Stitch Me Deadly
Thread Reckoning
The Long Stitch Goodnight
Thread on Arrival
Cross-Stitch Before Dying
Thread End
Wicked Stitch
The Stitching Hour
Better Off Thread

Writing as Gayle Trent

Cake Decorating Mystery Series

Murder Takes the Cake
Dead Pan
Killer Sweet Tooth
Battered to Death

Killer Wedding Cake

Myrtle Crumb Mystery Series

Between A Clutch and A Hard Place
When Good Bras Go Bad
Claus of Death
Soup...Er...Myrtle!
Perp and Circumstance

Stand Alone Books

In Her Blood
The Flame
The Perfect Woman

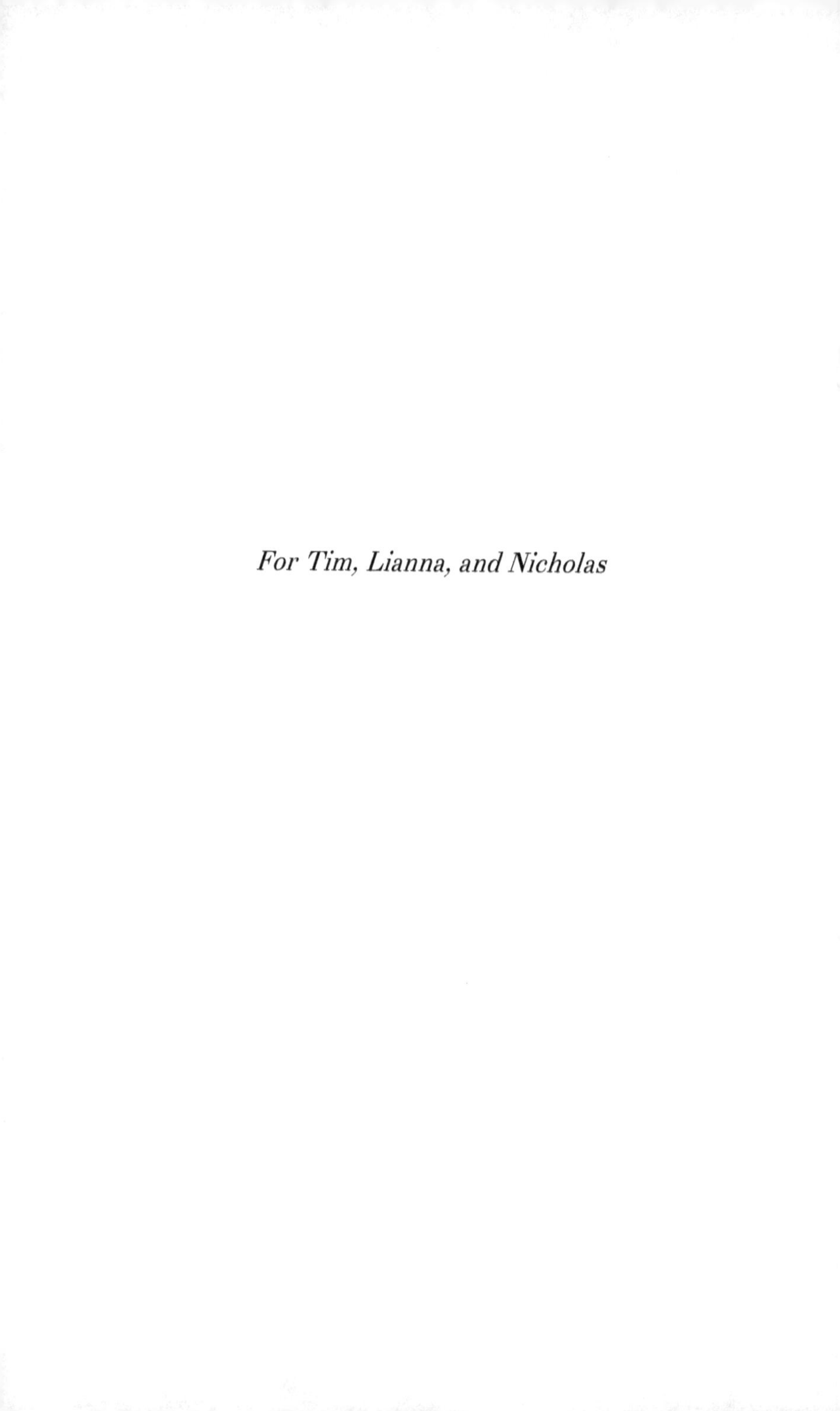

For Tim, Lianna, and Nicholas

You can have anything you want in life if you dress for it.

–EDITH HEAD

Chapter One

Seeing my best friend's disembodied head sticking through the wall was disconcerting.

"Look," Max said, poking her hands through the wall to frame her face. "I'm a big game trophy." She gave me a saucy grin and batted her eyes. "Take my photograph."

I dutifully picked up my phone, opened the camera feature, and took Max's picture.

She floated on into the room and peered at the image over my shoulder. As usual, Max had been reduced to a white flare on an otherwise bare spot on the wall.

"Nuts." She sighed. "Being a ghost has its drawbacks, you know."

I suppressed a smile. "I can imagine."

Maxine Englebright—Max—had died in 1930. Shops on Main had been her family home then. Max had been on her way to a dance—with my great, great-grandfather, oddly enough—had fallen down the stairs, and had broken her neck. She'd died instantly. And she was still wearing the mauve party dress and peacock-feather headband she'd had on as she'd taken her tumble. So, even though she'd been dead for nearly ninety years, it appeared she was still adjusting.

I did like to think I'd made Max's life—er, rather afterlife—a bit better. Since renting space at Shops on Main and opening my vintage-inspired fashion design boutique, Designs on You, Max had been introduced to the joys of technology. She was now enjoying books, movies, and television programs on her—formerly, my—tablet, so I didn't feel too sorry for her when she was pulling these crazy stunts and distracting me from my work.

"I've got to get this dress finished before Kristen gets here." I looked up at the clock across from my sewing machine. "And school will let out in less than two hours."

Max flicked her wrist. "No worries, darling. You've got this thing by the tail on a downhill pull. I don't know why Princess Kristen has to have a custom dress for the dance anyhow."

"Because she's spoiled, and custom dresses keep us in business," I reminded her.

She smiled. "There is that."

When I'd learned that Winter Garden's homecoming dance had a 1950s theme, I'd showcased some 50s-style dresses I already had in my ready-to-wear line on social media. I'd also gotten busy making more dresses and skirts in a variety of sizes and styles that would fit the theme. The items were selling well. But Kristen Holbrook had swept into Designs on You and had demanded a custom dress that would be "yellow with white trim, unlike any other dress that will be at the dance. I always stand out."

Together, Kristen and I had come up with what she had deemed the perfect dress.

After the young woman had left, Max had perched on the corner of my desk and said, "If we could buy that child for what she's worth and sell her for what she thinks she's worth, we'd make a killing." She'd referred to Kristen as "Princess Kristen" or simply "the princess" ever since.

"I think I'll duck out for a while," Max said. "I'll be back after the princess leaves."

"All right." I knew it took a lot of energy for Max to hang around as much as she did.

I was down to the hemming of the dress, so I put an adjustable blind hem foot on my sewing machine. I glanced around the atelier. I was proud of the progress I'd made in just a couple of months. The workshop was neatly laid out and contained three sewing machines, a long white worktable, a metal filing cabinet to store patterns, a full-length three-way mirror, and a custom shelf made by Grandpa. The shelf even sported an elaborately carved A at the top, and it was big enough to store bolts of fabric in the bottom and pattern books, sketchbooks, pens, and watercolor pencils in the top.

Two dress forms stood in the atelier. Sometimes Max liked to hover behind them and pretend she was trying on the outfits they wore. I'd push them over in front of the mirror so she could admire the clothes. It must be tough—especially for a fashionista like her—to have to wear the same outfit all the time.

There was an ornate Oriental screen separating the workshop from my reception room. Two navy wingback chairs flanked a small marble table in front of the window. I had a writing desk that faced the door, and a pair of mannequins stood in the room. One wore a 1950s-inspired polka dot, A-line dress and a black grosgrain hat, and the other modeled a Renaissance gown. Halloween would be here in a few weeks, and the gown was versatile enough to wear for a costume party as well as to a RenFaire, a masquerade ball, or a cosplay event.

Max and Grandpa Dave had been encouraging me to host an open house, but the time had never seemed right. One of the Shops on Main vendors had died just before I'd moved into my boutique, and it would have been in poor taste to throw a party then. I wasn't about to mention it to Max—and maybe not to Grandpa Dave, at least, not yet—but I was considering having a Halloween party. It would be an excellent way to showcase Designs on You and to introduce newcomers to my fashions. And Max would be absolutely over the moon. Being tethered to this building had done nothing to curb her curiosity and enthusiasm toward people. She'd love being in the middle of a soiree, even if Grandpa and I were the only ones who knew she was there.

I'd barely finished pressing Kristen's dress when the princess flounced into the boutique and flung herself onto one of the navy chairs. The theatrical movement was enough to make my cat Jasmine raise her gray and white striped head for a moment before repositioning herself on the windowsill and yawning at the rain.

"Hi, Kristen," I said. "Your dress is ready, if you'd like to try it on."

"Yeah." The word emerged from her lips as a sigh. "I need something to cheer me up today."

"Would you like to talk about it?" I asked.

"Of course, she wants to talk about it," Max said. "I thought for a moment she was going to have to throw herself onto the floor before you'd give her the response she wanted."

I pierced Max with a glare that plainly asked what she was doing here when she'd told me she'd be back after Kristen left.

The ghostly fashionista shrugged. "I couldn't stand it. I wanted to see the finished dress."

Fortunately, Kristen couldn't see or hear Max. In fact, other than Jazzy and me, no one else at Shops on Main seemed to be aware of her. And the only other person who could see and communicate with Max—as far as we knew—was Grandpa Dave.

"Our play is ruined," Kristen said, looking up at the ceiling. "Stupid Ms. Jessup is leaving us high and dry."

"Was she the play's director?" I couldn't imagine a teacher leaving her students in the lurch, but maybe it had been an emergency.

Kristen scoffed, as she brought her eyes back to mine. "No. She was a janitor, but she was in charge of costumes and props for the play."

"Why can't she still do that?" I asked. "I imagine she was being paid extra for the costuming job...unless it was a volunteer position."

"It wasn't volunteer, and she was being paid...well, I might add," Kristen said.

"Well enough to put up with you, Princess?" Max asked.

"I know because I saw the budget." Kristen examined her pink-tipped nails. "They say this polish is the color the Royals wear." She turned her hand toward me.

I ignored Kristen's comment about her nail polish and asked why Ms. Jessup's leaving the school necessitated her abandoning the play.

"It's because she's leaving the state. Her mom is sick, and she has to go take care of her."

"I'm so sorry to hear that," I said.

"Thanks." She blew out a breath. "You know...you could do it."

I frowned. "Do what?"

"Ka-thunk!" Max exclaimed. "That was the sound of the other shoe dropping."

"You could do the costumes." Kristen leaned forward as if this idea had just occurred to her, but neither Max nor I had been born yesterday. This entire performance had been carefully choreographed.

"What play are you doing?" I asked.

"*Beauty and the Beast*." Kristen beamed. "Naturally, I'm Belle."

"Naturally," Max parroted. "As if anyone else in the school—dare I say, world—could play the part."

Kristen opened her tiny designer purse and took out a card. "This is Ms. Kelly's number. She said to have you call anytime this afternoon to discuss the costuming with her." She stood. "I'd like to try on my dress now."

I walked Kristen to the front door of Shops on Main. She was carrying her dress, and I didn't want her to drop it trying to open the heavy door with her hands full.

"Don't forget to call Ms. Kelly!" Kristen called over her shoulder, as she stepped out onto the wood plank porch.

"I won't." I closed the door and smiled at Connie, who was standing in her doorway.

Connie owned Delightful Home, and it was located directly across the hall from Designs on You. Connie's shop smelled of cinnamon and sage, sometimes lavender, depending on the essential oils she was diffusing at the time. In addition to oils, Connie sold candles, soaps, lotions, and tea blends.

"I couldn't help overhearing," Connie said, pushing a strand of her long, honey blonde hair behind her ear. "My friend Susan has a child in Sandy's class—and who's also appearing in the senior play this fall. Sandra Kelly and I went to college together. Anyway, Susan told me the person who was heading up wardrobe and set design for the play has quit."

"Yes, that's what Kristen was telling me."

"You know, even if you can only help out a little, it would be a tremendous service to the school." Connie tilted her head, making the silver hoops in her earlobes glisten in the light. "And it would earn you the appreciation of the Winter Garden community."

I nodded. "I'll call Ms. Kelly and see what I can do." I went back to Designs on You.

"What's with this play—*Beauty and the Beast*?" Max asked. "Is it a fairy tale, like Snow White?"

"I'll show you." I went to the desk and opened the tablet Max used for reading and watching movies. I downloaded the animated version of the movie *Beauty and the Beast.* "They made a live-action version, but this is the first one I saw. I fell in love with it." I smiled. "Mom did too. She told me that the Beast was voiced by Robby Benson and that she had a major crush on him back in the day. She said she even still has a *Tiger Beat* with him on the cover."

"What's a *Tiger Beat*?"

I shrugged. "I guess it was a magazine back when Mom was a kid. I was always more into *Teen Vogue.*"

Max huffed. "All I had was *Motion Picture* and *Cosmopolitan.*"

My jaw dropped. "You read *Cosmopolitan*?"

She nodded. "It wasn't as exciting as *Motion Picture*, but the stories were pretty good."

After work, I put Jazzy and her cat carrier into the backseat. Jason's car wasn't in the lot, but I hadn't expected it to be. I knew he had to work late this evening. He'd been booked solid since before Labor Day, mostly with senior portraits.

Jason and I had been dating this past month. I knew it wasn't a good idea to get involved with someone who worked in the same building, but he and I had really been drawn to each other. He'd taken photos of me in some of my designs to help promote both our businesses, and our friendship had grown.

I opened the door of my tiny green SUV—SUV crossover, to be precise—and slid behind the steering wheel. It was just past five o'clock, and it was nearly dusk.

As soon as I'd backed out of my parking spot and started driving toward Main Street, I called Grandpa Dave. I'd always been closer to Grandpa—my dad's father—than I'd been to anyone. He lived about ten minutes away from us the whole time I was growing up. I still lived in my mom and dad's house. Dad had taken a job in Florida over two years ago.

Grandma Jodie had been dead just over five years, and especially since Mom and Dad had gone to Florida, Grandpa and I spent time together at least two or three times a week. I used my car's Bluetooth connection to call him, thinking he might like for me to bring dinner.

"Hi, Pup," he answered. "I hoped you'd call today."

"Well, I hope you're hungry. Jazzy and I are."

"That cat is always hungry. Then again, so am I." He chuckled. "And you're in luck. I have a turkey breast in the slow cooker."

"I am in luck," I said. "I was going to offer to bring something, but this is even better. Be there in a few."

Jasmine and I were such frequent visitors to Grandpa Dave's house that he always had some of her preferred cat food on hand. He always had my favorites on hand too. Mom and Dad thought Grandpa Dave spoiled me. He did. And we were both perfectly all right with that. Hopefully, I spoiled him too. I tried, anyway.

When I drove up the long driveway leading to Grandpa's house, I saw that he'd kept up Grandma

Jodie's tradition of putting a fodder shock, a friend-ly-looking scarecrow, and an uncarved pumpkin on the porch to herald the fall season. I was glad he hadn't put away the white rockers or taken down the swing yet—we still had some warm days left to enjoy those.

Grandpa came out onto the porch as I parked the car. I got out, opened the back door, and let Jazzy out of the cat carrier. She ran to the porch as quickly as she could. By the time I got to the porch, Grandpa Dave had already scooped her up, and she was nuzzling his chin.

"The porch looks nice," I said, as I strode up the steps and gave Grandpa a hug.

"Yeah, I didn't put the decorations out as early as Jodie would've, but I finally got around to it."

We went into the house, and I inhaled the mouth-watering aromas of cooking turkey, onion, and—

"Potatoes?" I asked.

He grinned. "Yep. All we need is the dressing. Will you do the honors while I feed Ms. Jasmine?"

"Gladly." I put my purse on a chair in the living room and went to the kitchen sink to wash my hands. I'd worn a fifties-style dress with a bolero jacket to-day, so I took the jacket off and put it with my purse.

"You'll get cold with those bare arms," Grandpa warned.

"Not if I stay busy."

I took a loaf of bread from the breadbox and retrieved a cookie sheet from beneath the oven. It was harder to make turkey dressing for just the two of us. After Grandma Jodie had died, I'd taken over making the dressing for family dinners. I had to be mindful of how much toast I was making when it was only the two of us. I buttered the bread and put it under the broiler.

"Did you have a good day today?" Grandpa asked.

"I did. Max made a spectacle of herself." I explained about her making herself appear to be a big game trophy, and he laughed.

"She is a sight," he said.

I then told him about Kristen and her wanting me to speak with her teacher about making costumes for the Winter Garden High School production of *Beauty and the Beast*.

"Are you going to do it?" he asked.

"I don't know." I sighed. "I'm concerned about taking on a project of that size."

"Eh, at least speak with the teacher and see what she says. By now, she might've recruited one of the moms or something."

"That's true." I put on potholders and took the toast out of the oven. "I'll call her after dinner."

"Funny you should mention Winter Garden," Grandpa said. "I'm taking part in the farmers' market there this weekend."

"Winter Garden has a farmers' market now?"

He nodded. "For one more week anyway. The Down South Café is hosting it in their parking lot."

"And you're taking some of your woodworking?"

"Yeah." He shrugged. "I doubt I'll sell anything, but it'll give me a chance to meet new people."

I shook my head. "You'll sell everything you take and come home with orders for more."

Grandpa just grinned. He knew I was right.

Grandpa and I tidied the kitchen, and then he looked at the clock. "You'd better call that teacher if you and I are going to watch something on television before you leave."

"All right." I went into the living room, retrieved my phone and the card Kristen had given me, and sank onto the black leather armchair near the fireplace. I slipped off my shoes and tucked my legs beneath me. I keyed in the number and half-hoped the call would go to voice mail. It didn't.

"Hello, this is Sandra Kelly."

"Hi, Ms. Kelly. I'm Amanda Tucker. Kristen Holbrook gave me your number."

"Ms. Tucker, I'm so glad you called. We're in a bit of a bind."

"Please call me Amanda," I said.

"Great. And call me Sandy. As I'm sure Kristen told you, we're putting on a production of *Beauty and the Beast*."

I laughed softly. "I'd imagine Kristen has told that to anyone who'll listen. She's very excited to be playing the role of Belle."

"Yes, she is. There's usually little to no budget for wardrobe and set design for a high school musical, but this is Kristen's senior year, and her parents want to ensure the child goes out with a bang," Sandy said. "So, while the amount is still modest, there is a budget in place."

"How much time do you think would be involved in an undertaking like this?" I asked. "I've never done costuming for a play before, and I do have a business to run."

"Of course, you do. And you certainly wouldn't be expected to do everything yourself. The Winter Garden parents are great about pitching in. We have a production meeting scheduled for tomorrow afternoon. If you'd be able to join us, we could discuss all the particulars and you could make your decision then."

"Sounds good."

"By the way, you don't happen to know anyone who could oversee the set design, do you?" Sandy asked.

I looked into the dining room where Grandpa Dave sat with Jazzy on his lap. He had his reading glasses perched on his nose and was staring down at a half-worked jigsaw puzzle.

"As a matter of fact," I told Sandy, "I just might know someone who'd be perfect for the job."

Chapter Two

ax wasn't in the shop when Jazzy and I got there the next morning. I imagined it had taken a lot of energy for her to be here long enough to watch the movie last night if she had, indeed, watched it all. She sometimes preferred to watch movies a section at a time. But, more often, she'd rather read.

I made sure both the entrance door from the foyer and the door leading to the kitchen were closed before I let Jasmine out of her carrier. I didn't want her to get out of Designs on You and disturb the other vendors, but I especially didn't want her to somehow get out the main door and onto the busy road.

I went into the kitchen to fill Jazzy's water bowl. Frank Peterman was there getting a cup of coffee. Frank was a jovial man of average height. He had a slight paunch, a bulbous nose, and brown hair that seemed to go in every direction at once. He and his wife Ella owned Everything Paper, a stationery shop.

"Good morning, Frank," I said.

"Hey, there. How's Dave doing?"

Frank and my grandfather had become friends since I'd moved into Shops on Main. Being one of only three male residents here, Frank was always happy when Grandpa Dave dropped by.

"He's doing great. I'm sure he'll be around before long."

I took the water back into the shop to find that Jazzy had already curled up on her bed in the atelier. She apparently found work boring without Max here to liven things up. I put some kibble in her food bowl and then got a sketchpad, some pencils, and my laptop before sitting down at the worktable.

Even though I still wasn't positive I'd be working on the play, I thought I'd like to have some idea about what I'd be committing to if I did sign on. For instance, I had no qualms about making Belle's or any of the other characters' wardrobes, and I guessed the school would either rent or buy a Beast costume. But how on earth would I go about creating a wardrobe, a feather duster, or a clock?

As I sat pondering this dilemma instead of doing my actual work, Trish Oakes strode into Designs on You after giving a brisk, perfunctory knock. Ms. Oakes had taken over the day-to-day management of

Shops on Main after Mrs. Meacham left to stay home and provide full-time care for her husband.

Ms. Oakes was a tall, severe-looking lady. Today, she was accompanied by a woman who reminded me of Elizabeth Taylor in her Father of the Bride days. I closed my laptop and joined the women in the reception area of my shop.

"Good morning, Amanda," Ms. Oakes said. "This is Carla Glenn. Ms. Glenn is considering our vacant space upstairs."

"That's great," I said. "What do you do, Carla?"

"I'm a massage therapist." Carla's voice was soft and throaty.

"Welcome to Shops on Main." I held out my hand, and Carla gave it a firm shake. "I'm Amanda Tucker, and as you can see, I'm a designer." I spread my arms slightly. "I create both ready-to-wear and one-of-a-kind pieces based on vintage patterns and styles."

"Interesting." Her gaze went to the canvas over my mantle.

The canvas displayed a photo Jason had taken of me in an emerald 1930s-style bias cut evening gown with a plunging halter neckline and a back panel with pearl buttons to the waist on each side. For this shot, Jason had asked me to turn and look at him over my shoulder.

Carla gave me an enigmatic smile. "Jason Logan, right?"

"Yes. Do you know Jason?"

"I used to," she said. "Too bad he isn't here right now. I'll have to try to catch him later."

"That Dumb Dora better not try to steal your man," Max said from somewhere in the vicinity of my right shoulder. "If she does, she'll have me to reckon with."

"You'll have plenty of opportunities to see Jason if you lease the space," Ms. Oakes told Carla.

"Maybe so, but he'll give you the icy mitt and tell you to go chase yourself!" Max was awfully wound up about this situation, and I couldn't quite follow her terminology.

Before I could stop myself, I blurted, "Icy mitt?"

Both Carla and Ms. Oakes looked at me as if I'd sprouted horns.

I gave an uncomfortable chuckle. "You'll have to excuse me. I'm completely absorbed in my work this morning."

"You're making icy mitts?" Ms. Oakes asked.

"Mittens." I waved my hand. "For a costume. Anyway, nice to meet you, Carla."

"It was a pleasure meeting you too." Carla turned toward the door.

With one last look of puzzlement flung in my direction, Ms. Oakes followed her. Thankfully, she remembered to close the door behind her because now that Max was in the shop, Jazzy was sitting on the floor looking up at her adoringly.

"Hello, my darling," Max said to the cat.

When I heard the women's voices across the hall at Delightful Home, I put my hands on my hips and glared at Max. "What have I told you about sneaking up on me?"

"You told me not to do it, but I can't help it. I'm a ghost. Stealth is kinda my thing."

"Not when I'm having a conversation with someone else, it isn't."

She gave me a shrug/head-tilt combo. "Sorry, but I simply couldn't help myself. That old sourpuss Oakes telling that dame—who made it clear that she knows your Jason—that she could see him anytime if she leases the shop? Why, that flew all over me! It's as if Sourpuss is using your fella as bait to get that Dorothy Gish wannabe to rent the shop."

I remembered that Dorothy Gish was a silent film star, but I still had no idea what "give you the icy mitt and tell you to go chase yourself" meant. Although, given that Max was pacing and flailing her arms as she ranted, I could make an educated guess.

She thought that if Carla tried to lure Jason away from me, he'd give her the cold shoulder and tell her to get lost. I wasn't as confident about Jason's loyalty as Max either was or wanted me to believe she was. After all, he and I had only been dating for a short time, and Carla had made it obvious that she and Jason shared a past.

Max had gone to see what Sourpuss and Dorothy Gish were up to, and I was back in front of the laptop trying to figure out how to make costumes for furniture and home accessories that kids could move around in...preferably in relative comfort and with the ability to see and breathe freely.

I was lost in thought and started when there was a sharp rap on the door between the atelier and the kitchen. I looked up as Ella Peterman barreled into the workroom.

The petite woman was livid. "I absolutely do not want that floozy coming here and opening up her massage parlor."

I stood and went around the side of the table. "I don't think Carla would be doing anything inappropriate. Surely, Ms. Oakes wouldn't allow that."

"Not illegal, but I wouldn't put inappropriate past either one of them." She smoothed her short salt-and-pepper hair. "If she moves in, Frank and I are moving out. He doesn't know that yet, but I'm sticking to my guns."

Patting Ella's shoulder, I said, "Everything will be okay."

"No, it won't. I've had run-ins with her kind before. A woman like that broke up my mother and father's marriage."

What in the world could Carla have done to give Ella the impression that she was on the verge of wrecking the poor woman's marriage? I decided maybe some logic would help to diffuse Ella's anxiety.

"Ella, she can't put a massage therapy office on the second floor of a building that has no elevator. How would someone in pain navigate those stairs?"

She brightened. "That's an excellent point. I wonder if she's thought of it?"

"I'm sure she has." I smiled. "I'm guessing she's only allowing Ms. Oakes to show her around the place to humor her."

Ella nodded. "You know, I bet you're right. You're a clever girl." She squeezed my arm. "I'd better get back to Frank."

Max popped in a few minutes later, and I told her about Ella's visit.

"I have no idea what Carla did to her, but if—and I quote—'that floozy' sets up shop upstairs, Ella and Frank are leaving."

"I know what Carla did," Max said. "I saw the whole thing. Carla went sashaying into Everything Paper with that boom-chicka-boom walk of hers." She treated me to an exaggerated demonstration. "Frank's mouth dropped open, and his chewing gum fell out. It landed in the open cash drawer and got stuck to a dollar bill. Mr. Smooth was trying to look nonchalant and get the gum off the dollar, and he tore the thing in half."

I laughed. "Poor Frank."

"When I left, he was trying to tape that dollar back together while sneaking a peek at old Boom-Chicka-Boom flouncing back out."

I had a feeling that Frank Peterman was going to be in the doghouse for quite a while.

Grandpa Dave came into Designs on You at around three-thirty that afternoon.

"Hi, Pup!" he called, as he closed the door behind him.

Jazzy languidly stood, stretched, and strolled over to him. He picked her up, and she rubbed the top of her head against his chin.

I smiled. "Have you had a good day so far, Grandpa?"

"So far, so good. How about you?"

"I'm fine. I think your buddy Frank has had a fairly rough day though," I said.

"Why's that?" he asked.

Before I could answer, Max popped in to do the honors. "He let a showy dame turn his head, and Ella didn't appreciate it one iota." She winked. "Hey, there, Silver Fox."

Silver fox was a term Max had heard from a woman who used to work upstairs, and she'd decided the moment she met Grandpa Dave that the term suited him.

"Hello, Max." He placed Jazzy back onto the floor. "Who was this showy dame?"

"A massage therapist who was talking with Ms. Oakes about leasing the vacant space." I began to tidy my desk as I spoke. "She reminded me of a young Liz Taylor."

"I hate I missed her then," he said.

I looked up in time to see Max swatting at Grandpa Dave. Of course, she couldn't touch him, but she managed to get her point across.

"What?" he asked, looking from Max to me and back again. "Did I say something wrong?"

"No. It's just that—" I cleared my throat. "The...um...dame...made it clear that she knew Jason."

"Your Jason?"

"Yes, her Jason!" Max exclaimed.

I huffed. "He's not really mine, you know. I don't own the man."

Neither of them paid attention to me.

"And she wasn't even all that pretty." Max tossed her head. "She was no Olive Thomas, believe you me. But, oh, she thought she was. The way she sashayed into Everything Paper, you'd have thought she was being played onto the stage by a trombone and a drummer." She told Grandpa how Carla had made Frank drop his gum.

Grandpa laughed. "I'll have to go check on him before Amanda and I leave. Tell me more about this Olive Thomas. She must've been something special if she could outshine Elizabeth Taylor."

"I don't know that Elizabeth bird—you two will have to introduce me later—but Olive was a shooting star who died tragically and far too young."

The irony of Max's words was apparently lost on her. She'd died before she was thirty years old herself.

"How Dot and I wept when we heard about it," Max continued. "Poor Olive was on her honeymoon in Paris, and even though the authorities ruled her death an accident, the public speculated that it might've been suicide...or murder." She wandered over to the mantle. "I can remember sitting with Dot in this very room talking about Olive."

She seemed to be a million miles away then, and Grandpa and I exchanged glances.

"I believe I'll check on Frank," Grandpa said quietly, "and see if he has time to have a cup of coffee with me in the kitchen."

I nodded. "While you're doing that, I'll straighten up the atelier."

A few minutes later, I noticed that Max had moved from the reception area into the workroom and was sitting atop the filing cabinet.

"I certainly brought down the room, didn't I?" she asked.

"Are you all right?"

She nodded. "I still miss my baby sister. How I wish I could know what became of her."

"Would you like me to try to find out?"

Max's eyes widened. "You could do that?"

"Yes. With enough information, I believe I can." I held up a hand. "I have to warn you, though. We have no idea what direction Dorothy's life might've taken."

"I don't care," Max said. "I still want to know...no matter what. What do you need to know before you can find her?"

I picked up my phone so I could text myself the information. "What's your sister's full name and date of birth?"

"Dorothy Ann Englebright, born October 16, 1914." Her eyes sparkled. "You're going to find Dot. I know you are."

I doubted I'd find Dot exactly. After all, the woman would be well over a century old at this point if she was still living. So, unless Max's sister was haunting some other house in Abingdon, I felt sure I wouldn't discover Dot herself. But, hopefully, I could learn what had happened to her and report back to Max that her sister had lived a long and happy life.

By the time Grandpa Dave returned, Max was gone. I wondered if these past couple of days had taxed her energy or if she'd left us to be alone with her thoughts.

Other than an exaggerated eyebrow raise, Grandpa didn't give me any indication of how his conversation with Frank had gone. I knew we'd talk about it once we were on the road.

I loaded Jazzy into her carrier, and Grandpa Dave turned off the lights and made sure the door to the reception area was locked. We were leaving by the workshop door today.

"Is Frank still in trouble with Ella?" I asked, as we drove toward Winter Garden High School.

"He says he isn't, but he kept glancing over his shoulder and didn't linger over his coffee for too long." Grandpa gave a soft chuckle. "I imagine that would've been quite a sight to see—Frank dropping his chewing gum into the cash register."

"Max seemed to have enjoyed it."

Grandpa looked into the backseat at the cat carrier. "Are you sure you want to take Jazzy along to this meeting? We have time to go by the house and drop her off."

"Actually, we don't." I checked the rearview mirror to reassure myself that Jazzy was contentedly lying in her carrier enjoying the ride. "I want to get there in time to speak with Ms. Kelly before the meeting begins."

"Okay, but if you get in trouble for bringing your pet to school, don't think I'm going to bail you out."

"I'll say I brought her for show-and-tell," I said.

Walking into a high school gymnasium—even at this stage of my life—gave my stomach a flutter of apprehension. Memories of past crushes, struggling through the Presidential Fitness Test, and pretending to be unaffected by the exclusion from certain cliques made me feel like an awkward thirteen-year-old again. I reminded myself that I was a grown woman now...and an entrepreneur to boot, and I held my head high. What difference did it make that I was with my grandpa and was carrying my kitty in a pink pet carrier? Just because I was a strong, independent woman now didn't mean I had to get carried away and forego all my comforts.

Sandra Kelly was an angular woman, and her platinum hair had darker blonde streaks. She wore a charcoal gray business suit and no-nonsense black heels. As soon as she looked up from the clipboard she was holding, she waved at Grandpa Dave and me and hurried in our direction.

"Hi!" She thrust out her hand. "You must be Amanda. I'm Sandy."

I shook Sandy's hand and introduced her to Grandpa. "Sandy, this is my grandfather, Dave Tucker."

"Our set design genius?" she asked.

I ignored the look of mild outrage Grandpa shot my way and answered the question. "He certainly is. He does amazing work."

"I wouldn't go that far," Grandpa said. "I've never designed a set before."

"There's a first time for everything," Sandy said. "And we have a fabulous group of volunteers who are eager to help you out—both of you." She smiled. "You'll be meeting them all soon." She was distracted by someone coming through the door. "Excuse me, please. Oh, and welcome to the team!"

As Sandy marched off to speak with the newcomer, Grandpa Dave widened his eyes at me. "I thought we were simply coming to check out this situation. I didn't realize you'd already signed us up."

"Neither did I." I shrugged. "We can still back out, though...right?"

"Let's have a seat and make our minds up following this meeting," he said.

As we found two vacant folding chairs placed in front of the stage, I knew Grandpa and I were thinking the same thing: at this point, if we declined, Sandra Kelly would make us feel as if we were quitting and letting down her students.

A young woman placed her frayed backpack on the chair beside Grandpa Dave. She jabbed a thumb in my direction. "She with you?"

I turned my head and gave her a pointed look. "I can hear you, you know."

"I know." She grinned. "You're just pretty eccentric sitting there in your fifties' fashion model dress with your big pink cat carrier by your side. You might be a supervillain for all I know." She looked at Grandpa. "Is she?"

"Only on Wednesdays," he said.

It was Wednesday.

She laughed. "I like you."

"I'm Amanda Tucker," I said.

"And I'm her grandfather, Dave." He shook the girl's hand.

"Zoe Flannagan, stage manager, student, uncelebrated genius." She nodded at me. "I'm guessing you're the designer."

"Good guess."

"So you're gonna help us pull this thing off?" she asked.

I smiled. "I sure am."

I didn't know what it was about this sassy teen with her skinny jeans, black t-shirt, and high-top sneakers that made me decide to help out with this production. But whatever it was, the charming little enchantress used the same spell on Grandpa.

"I'm helping too," he said. "My specialty is set design."

My specialty he says, like he's a Broadway veteran.

Sandra Kelly approached the stage as the chairs around us continued filling up. A balding man with thick glasses caught up to her before she mounted the steps. I couldn't tell what was being said, but it was obvious Sandy wasn't happy at being disturbed, and she didn't want to talk with him.

I leaned across Grandpa so I could ask Zoe, "Who's he?"

"Fergus Kramer," she said. "He's the school bookkeeper."

"Ah, he holds the purse strings for this production?" Grandpa asked.

Zoe nodded. "That and everything else around here."

I imagined everyone in the area of the stage heard Sandra when she firmly told Mr. Kramer, "We will discuss this later."

Red faced, Mr. Kramer avoided looking at the meeting participants as he stormed out of the auditorium. I'd have thought as the person in charge of the budget, Mr. Kramer should have stayed for the meeting. But, then, what did I know?

I was soon to learn that I didn't know much at all about what happened behind the scenes of a high school musical production.

Chapter Three

I drove Grandpa back to Shops on Main to get his truck. All the windows in the brick Victorian house were dark, and I didn't see Max at any of them.

"Would you like to go back in and see if she's there?" Grandpa asked. He had this uncanny ability to read my mind.

"No. I really need to get home."

"Yeah, me too."

"I forgot to mention it earlier, but while you were talking with Frank, I agreed to look into Dorothy's life...to see if I can discover what happened to her," I said.

"Dorothy? Max's sister?" he asked.

I nodded.

"Are you sure you're up to the task, Pup?"

"I am." I ran my hand over my forehead. "But I desperately hope Dorothy enjoyed a long and happy life. Max got so sad today when she was talking about Dot...I don't want to have to give her any tragic news about the woman."

"Max is tough. She can handle the truth about Dorothy, no matter what it is." He kissed my cheek and opened the car door. "Goodnight, ladies. I've got to go home and try to figure out how to design a balcony a child can pretend to fall from and not get hurt."

"Goodnight, Grandpa."

I waited until he was in his truck with the engine started before pulling out of the parking lot. I took one last look at the Shops on Main windows but still saw no sign of Max. Not for the first time, I wondered where she went when she wasn't with us.

At home, I ate a grilled cheese sandwich and sketched a dress fit for an enchanted feather duster. It wasn't a difficult design—a mermaid-style black dress with black and gray panels made to look like feathers that would swish from the knees to the ankles when the character walked. I added a headband with two corresponding plumes—one gray and one black—on the left side.

My phone rang. When I plucked it out from under a box of coloring pencils, I saw that it was Jason.

"Hey, there," I said. "You must be having a busy day. I didn't see your car at Shops on Main at all."

"You're right. I didn't make it into the studio today. I've been going from one location to the next until…well, until now, as a matter of fact. Have you had dinner?"

"I have, but I'd love some company. If you'd like to stop by, I'll be happy to make a grilled cheese sandwich and some tomato soup for you."

"Thanks," he said. "I'm on my way."

While I waited for Jason, I prepared the light meal I'd promised him. I was plating the sandwich when he arrived.

I gave him a quick kiss hello. "Perfect timing."

He sat down at the kitchen table. "Thank you for doing this."

"You're welcome." I sat the plate in front of him and poured the tomato soup into a bowl. "You look exhausted."

"Gee, thanks. That's what every guy wants to hear from a beautiful woman."

"I didn't say you look bad. I said you look exhausted." I got a spoon from the silverware drawer. "Would it help if I said that, even tired, you still look handsome?"

He grinned. "It helps immensely."

With his dark, wavy hair and ocean blue eyes, I didn't know how he could ever look anything less than gorgeous.

He glanced over at my sketchpad. "Um...what are you making?"

"What does it look like?"

"Oh, no. That's a trap. I'm tired, but I haven't lost my mind," he said.

"I give you full immunity—I promise."

He raised his eyes warily and shook his head.

"Please," I said. "Tell me the first thing that comes to your mind when you look at that dress."

Jason bit his sandwich to avoid answering.

"If you'll tell me, there's a brownie in it for you." I waited.

Swallow. Grimace. Sigh. "A feather duster. It looks like a feather duster."

I gave a squeal of delight before I stood and hugged him.

"You're glad?" he asked.

"Thrilled." I laughed. "One of my clients—Kristen Holbrook—all but volunteered me to help with the costumes for Winter Garden High School's production of *Beauty and the Beast*."

"I know Kristen," Jason said. "I'm doing her senior portraits...and pretty much chronicling her final year of high school. I know how persuasive that young lady can be."

"Yeah. I went to a meeting tonight to find out more about the project and to see if I might be interested in making time to help." I indicated the sketch. "And now here I am costuming a feather duster."

Jason spread his hands. "If you don't have time, be firm. I like Kristen and her parents—they're nice people—but they have a way of acting like they're your only clients."

"Believe me, I know." I stopped myself just before I told Jason that Max referred to Kristen as the princess. It was hard sometimes to keep my best friend secret from Mr. I-Don't-Believe-in-Ghosts Logan. "But I love a challenge, and I think this will be fun."

"You nailed the feather duster." He crumbled saltines into his soup.

"I met a friend of yours today." I looked at the sketchpad as I spoke and concentrated on keeping my tone light.

"You mean Carla?" he asked. "She told me she was coming by."

"Yeah, she was with Ms. Oakes...checking the place out." I flipped over a fresh sheet on the pad. "She seemed interested in the available space, but I'm not sure it's practical for her to be on the second floor. I'm sure some massage therapy clients would have trouble navigating those stairs."

"Good point." Jason contemplated this while eating his soup. "Do you think anyone on the ground floor would consider switching with her?"

Had I been the one eating soup, I might've spit it across the table when he said that. "I don't believe any of us would be willing to give up our prime real estate. Connie and I count on our merchandise being visible in those large front windows, and the Petermans—" I decided not to mention Ella's concerns about Carla. Instead, I said, "I can't imagine they'd be willing to give up their easy access to the kitchen and the parking lot in order to trudge up and down stairs all day."

"That's true. Oh, well, I'm sure Carla will find a place somewhere." He nodded toward my sketchpad. "What's next?"

"The candlestick," I said. "I'm starting with the easiest—besides the dresses—and working up to the harder designs."

After Jason had finished eating and had put his dishes in the dishwasher, I asked him if he was up for a movie.

"Not a movie. I have to go home and check on Rascal."

Rascal was his "little white mutt." I hadn't had the pleasure of meeting the dog yet, but I hoped to soon.

"My neighbor feeds and walks him if I'm going to be late," Jason continued. "But I still need to spend some time with him. I feel guilty when I work the kind of hours I've been working lately and have to leave him."

"Can't you take him with you on shoots?"

"I guess I could, but it would be hard to watch him and concentrate on my work too." He slid his arms around my waist. "I still have a few minutes to beat you in a game show or something."

I smiled up at him. "Oh, you think you can beat me? The reigning trivia queen? In your dreams."

After Jason had gone home to tend to Rascal, I finished the sketch of the candlestick costume. Then I revisited the idea of the wardrobe, teapot, clock, and cup. At least, that's what I told myself I was doing. In reality, I was sitting on my sofa with my cat sleeping on my lap while I stared at a blank sheet of paper.

I tried to think about the costume designs, but it was a lot easier to dwell on Jason and Carla. It didn't bother me—okay, it didn't bother me as much—that they likely had a romantic relationship in the past. What concerned me was their current relationship. Jason spoke about Carla casually, but he'd been the one who'd recommended the vacant space at Shops on Main to her. And then he'd suggested to me that one of the other vendors might be willing to give up their space for her! As if! I couldn't help but wonder if he'd made the comment as a joke...or to get a rise out of me. Or was it because he truly wanted to work near her that badly? I was looking forward to discussing the matter with Max in the morning and getting her opinion.

Unfortunately, Max wasn't the first person I saw upon arriving at Shops on Main Thursday morning. That distinction fell to Ford, the burly, bearded proprietor of Antiquated Editions. I liked Ford, but I wasn't in the mood for his flippant handling of the topic I wanted to discuss with Max. And I hadn't even had my coffee yet.

Leaning against the kitchen sink, Ford looked as if he was just waiting for someone to come in so he could ask, "What did you think of our new compatri-ot?"

I stiffened as I reached for the coffee pot. "Did Ms. Oakes say Carla has signed the lease?"

"No, but she introduced her to all of us. I took that to mean it was practically a fait accompli."

Before I could respond, Ella walked into the kitchen.

"If you ask me, that woman is trouble with a capital T." Ella punctuated her statement with a firm nod. "If she moves in here, then Frank and I will be moving out."

It occurred to me that if Frank and Ella moved out, their downstairs space would be available for Carla.

"Please do don't that," I said to Ella. "This town needs Everything Paper. Right, Ford?"

"Sure," he said. "But I don't know why we can't have Everything Paper and the cute massage thera-pist too."

"Because we can't, that's why." Ella abruptly turned and left without her coffee.

"Go apologize," I hissed at Ford. "And take her some coffee."

"Apologize for what? I didn't do anything."

"You must have." I handed him an empty mug. "She left without her coffee."

"Fine." He sighed. "But I didn't do anything."

"He was insensitive," Max said after Ford left the kitchen. "You know it, I know it, and if he doesn't know it, he's a sap." She folded her arms. "Hurry up and get a wiggle on. I want to talk with you without people thinking you're goofy."

She disappeared, and I knew she'd gone to wait for me at Designs on You. I put sugar and creamer into my coffee and hurried back to the shop.

"I don't like it when you're mopey." Max was sitting on the worktable. "You're better than that."

"Who said I was being mopey?"

Max rolled her eyes. "Darling, I've been dead almost three times longer than I was alive. I've had plenty of time to study human behavior. And you're being mopey."

"Okay...maybe I am being a little mopey."

"You gonna give me the rumble, or are you just going to sit there?" she asked.

"You already know the rumble... or the story... or whatever rumble means. It's Carla. I don't want her working here any more than Ella does." I told Max about my conversation with Jason.

"He's screwy if he thinks any of the downstairs vendors would give up their keen spots."

"Maybe he was kidding," I said. "Or trying to see how I'd react."

"It sounds like you handled yourself fine. Don't give Jason and that overripe tomato another thought. After all, it was you he came to visit last night."

I smiled. "Yeah, it was."

"Tell me about your meeting at the school," she said. "Are you going to do the play?"

"I am. So is Grandpa. We were impressed with Sandra Kelly and with everything she, the students, and the parents spoke about at the meeting. But we were both especially taken with the stage manager, a kid named Zoe."

"Will I get to meet this gal?" She shrugged. "You know what I mean."

"I hope so. Grandpa and I have an idea."

"Let's hear it."

"We thought we could live stream some of the preparations and practices," I said.

Max looked blank.

I tried to explain a little better. "We could do a live video from the school and you could watch from here using your tablet."

She gasped. "Are you razzing me—trying to make me think that tablet is like the Beast's magic mirror?"

"It is," I said. "Or, at least, it can be, if someone sets it up. Maybe we can show you later."

Jazzy hopped onto the table and rolled onto her back near Max.

"Hello, my gorgeous darling," Max cooed. "Were we neglecting you?"

"How could we ever neglect you, Jasmine?" I wheeled my cart of art supplies over to the worktable. "You wouldn't let us. I still have to figure out how to make the bulkier costumes like the wardrobe."

There was a tap on the door between the atelier and the kitchen before Connie stepped into the room. "Good morning. I thought I heard you speaking to someone."

Jazzy emitted a low purp, rolled over, and leaped off the table.

"I think you've offended her," I said, with a laugh.

The cat strolled over and wound around Connie's ankles once before visiting her food bowl.

"How did the meeting go yesterday afternoon?" Connie asked.

"It went well. I'm heading up the costuming." I gestured at the blank sketch pad. "Any clue on how to create a wardrobe outfit? Jazzy was no help whatsoever."

Connie's brows knit together, and she rubbed her forehead. She was wearing a tie-dye red and pink tunic with black leggings, and she had a skinny braid hanging down in front of her left shoulder. She looked the part of a guru today. I was eager to see if she'd be able to offer me any insights. Fortunately for me, she was.

"There's a woman from New Jersey who has a costume shop on Etsy," Connie said. "Her name is Debra. I messaged her about a costume I was making for my youngest." She pulled a chair over from one of the sewing machines and sat as she warmed to the topic.

Max waved goodbye and vanished.

Connie continued her narrative. "I'd have ordered the costume pre-made, but I didn't have time. Ethan told me that afternoon, 'Oh Mama, I need to be an American flag in the school play tomorrow. Sorry, I forgot to tell you.' You'll see one of these days." She grinned as she shook her head. "You can't imagine the panic I was in."

"Oh, I think I can," I said. "I'd have been tempted to paint a flag on a t-shirt and send him on."

"And that would have been perfectly fine, but I have a tendency to overthink things." She laughed. "Especially when I go into Super Mom mode."

"Was Debra able to give you any pointers?"

"She was. She told me to use felt. It's stiff but easier to work with than some other materials. And she also told me to think about the costume as if it were a box. After that, creating a flag was simple." She frowned slightly. "But I'm not sure how you can apply that concept to a wardrobe."

"Like this." I sketched a box onto the paper and then added panels on each side. "These can open to reveal painted clothing, and we could even have a slit or two in here where the actor inside the costume could toss out of scarf or something." I smiled at her. "Connie, you're brilliant."

"Not me. The box idea was all Debra, and I love your thoughts on embellishing it. Oh, I almost forgot to mention it," she said. "Sandy has indicated an interest in recruiting the middle school drama club as extra villagers for the play, so my daughter Marielle might be participating."

"That's fantastic."

"I know. It's a wonderful opportunity for the younger students." She stood and pushed the chair back to its original location. "I'd better get back to Delightful Home. And don't worry about becoming overwhelmed with the costuming stuff. Several of the moms, including me, are willing to help out."

"Thanks," I said. "I truly appreciate that."

Chapter Four

Later that morning, I was sewing a zipper in a cocktail dress that I'd made for a client to wear to a formal affair. There was a sharp rap on the door, and Ms. Oakes strolled in. There was an older gentleman with her. He was tall and thin, and he wore a gray seersucker suit, white shirt, red bow tie, and white shoes.

"Hello, Amanda," Ms. Oakes said. "I'd like for you to meet Mr. Bare. Mr. Bare owns a business called Ticklish Taxidermy, and he's thinking about leasing the space upstairs." She lifted her chin as if daring me to make a disparaging comment about the name of Mr. Bare's shop.

While I must admit to having a disparaging thought or two about Ticklish Taxidermy, I wasn't about to give voice to them in front of Mr. Bare. I pushed my chair back from the sewing machine, walked over, and extended my hand. "Good morning, Mr. Bare. It's nice to meet you."

"Please call me Teddy." He smiled. "I call my business Ticklish Taxidermy because I try to make all of the animals look happy. Some even appear to be smiling or laughing." He took out his phone to show me some photographs.

Not even my disparaging thoughts had prepared me for this. The first picture was of a squirrel, mouth open wide, as it embraced a cluster of walnuts. Mr. Bare swiped this photo away, and his screen filled with the image of an owl in a graduation cap. He swiped again to show me a photograph of a deer. The creature's mouth was forming a creepy smile.

"That's Benji. He's my favorite," Mr. Bare said. "Benji isn't for sale. I enjoy having him with me too much. Every day I come in and look at that sweet smile and say 'Hello, my deer!' Get it?" He chuckled. "What do you think? Aren't they wonderful?"

"Um...I've never seen anything like them." That much was true.

"They're wonderfully awful," Max said from behind me. "Those are the most hideous things I've ever seen."

"Now, don't think these animals were killed in order for me to make my art." Mr. Bare put away his phone. "Absolutely not. I only make art from animals that died of natural causes."

"I'm so relieved to hear that," I said. "And, if you choose to lease the space, I'll look forward to working with you."

"Likewise, I am absolutely sure, young lady." Mr. Bare gave me a little bow.

"Yes, well, we'd better move along, Mr. Bare," Ms. Oakes said.

"Nice meeting you." I was able to hold in my laughter until after I heard Ms. Oakes' footsteps crossing the hall to Delightful Home. Then Max and I chortled.

"What in the world was that?" she asked.

"I think you said it best when you said it was wonderfully awful." I wiped my eyes. "But, at least, the animals died of natural causes before...well before."

"And still, Teddy Bare, the taxidermist, is a thousand times better than having Carla move in here," Max said.

"I guess. I just feel like it might be unsettling to have all those dead animals around."

Max snorted. "Says the woman who's talking to a ghost."

"Yeah, but you aren't scary in the slightest. You're charming."

My phone rang, and it was Sandra Kelly.

"Hi, Sandy," I said. "What can I do for you?"

"I realize it's last minute, and I understand if you can't today, but I'd really love to take you to lunch. Is there any possibility that you're free?"

I didn't like to close my shop during the day, but I had said yes to this project and I intended to give it my all. "Sure. When and where would you like to meet?"

"I don't have a very long lunch break," Sandy said. "Would you mind meeting at the Down South Café at eleven-forty?"

"That'll be fine. I'll look forward to seeing you then." I looked around for Max, but she'd vamoosed. I imagined she was following around Mr. Bare to see what other peculiarities he was showing to the other vendors.

Once I'd finished sewing in the zipper and pressing the dress, I went over to Delightful Home to tell Connie about my lunch plans.

"I hope I don't miss any clients, but I don't have any appointments scheduled. And it's early in the day. Hopefully, any browsers will come back. I'll mention the middle school drama club to Sandra Kelly to make sure she's planning on them taking part in the play."

"Thank you. I appreciate that." Connie toyed with the braid that fell over her left shoulder. "What did you think of the latest contender for the vendor spot?"

"Mr. Bare is certainly interesting." I tried to keep my voice sounding nonchalant. "Does this mean that Carla didn't take the space?"

"I'm not sure," Connie said. "Ms. Oakes does things differently from Mrs. Meacham. Melba waited until the lease was signed before she introduced the new vendor to anyone. Maybe Ms. Oakes wants to know right away if she can expect any conflicts among the vendors." She shrugged.

"Maybe. It makes sense."

At eleven-thirty-five, I walked into the Down South Cafe in Winter Garden. The cafe was as adorable as I'd remembered. The walls were a sunny yellow trimmed in blue. A refrigerated display case containing all sorts of luscious treats was near the cash register. I thought I would get something to take to Grandpa this afternoon before I left.

"Hey, there. What can I get for you?" The waitress who'd approached the table was wearing a blue Down South Café t-shirt and jeans. Her copper hair had been pulled back into a ponytail and secured with a yellow scrunchie.

I recognized Jackie from the last time Grandpa Dave and I had eaten here. "I'm waiting for someone, but I'd love a cup of coffee while I wait."

"Sure thing."

Sandra Kelly came through the door while Jackie was getting my coffee. Today, she wore a red pencil skirt, black kitten heels, and a black-and-red print blouse. I thought she looked more businesswoman than teacher, and I wondered if she was working toward an administrative position.

As she sat at the table, Sandra said, "Thank you for taking time away from your busy schedule and your shop not only to meet with me now but to take on costuming for the musical."

"You're welcome." I smiled. "I'm happy for the opportunity."

She reached into her purse and took out a list of names and phone numbers. "These are some parents who have volunteered to help with sewing, scene construction, snacks...whatever we might need."

Jackie returned with two cups of coffee. "Hi, Sandy. Do you guys know what you're having for lunch?"

I ordered the brunch quiche, and Sandra asked for a chef's salad.

"Connie, who owns Delightful Home, the shop next to mine, mentioned that you were considering using middle school drama students to play the villagers in the play," I said.

"Yes, we are extending roles to the middle school drama club because we're a small school and don't have enough students to fill the roles. They'll all need simple costumes, but they won't require a lot of practicing. So, don't worry that there'll be a horde of extra kids running around the stage in the school—a liability nightmare—all that often. And, of course, there will always be staff members on hand, but middle school staff will be there when their students are present too."

"I think it's fantastic that you're including the middle schoolers. I'm sure those children are thrilled to be a part of a high school production."

"I think it will be good practice for them. Plus, there is one talented elementary school upperclassman who will be playing Chip, the teacup. We thought it would be great if we could get a ten- or eleven-year-old for the role, and one of our middle schoolers has the most adorable little cousin. His name is Joey. Isn't that cute?"

Joey. Why does that name ring a bell to me? But I put that thought aside as Sandra continued to talk.

"I'll be a few minutes late to rehearsal this evening, so I might miss getting to see you and Dave today. But Zoe can help you out with anything you need. That young lady is such a little dynamo. I'd be lost without her." She sipped her coffee. "I believe she has a sad homelife, but she doesn't let that inhibit her."

"Why do you think her life is sad?" I asked.

"It's a feeling more than anything else." Sandra gave an elegant shrug. "It's like some days she'd do almost anything to avoid going home."

On the way back to the shop from the Down South Café, I got a call from Ruby Mills. Ruby had been one of my first clients—I'd made a dress for her to wear to her granddaughter's wedding. Now Ruby was going on vacation and needed a formal dress. With Ruby leaving on Tuesday, we both knew I had to work fast.

As soon as I got back into Designs on You, I got out Ruby's muslin pattern and sketch of the dress I'd made her for the wedding. Quickly sketching an A-line dress with a V-neck and below-the-knee hemline, I added sheer black lace sleeves and an inset to go over the neckline. I thought it would be beautiful on Ruby. I texted her with the design and started playing around with the design for the *Beauty and the Beast* teacup costume while I waited for her feedback.

Jason stuck his head in the doorway of the atelier. "Hello, gorgeous."

"Hi, handsome." I smiled and waved my hand around like a game show model. "Is there anything here I could interest you in?"

"Do you have any sugar to get me through the rest of the day?"

I thought I heard a gasp, but I decided to ignore it. Standing and walking around the worktable, I said, "Come on in and close that door, and we'll see what I've got."

He pushed the door closed, and we kissed.

"That should keep me going through my next appointment, but I might need a little more by the end of the day. Are you free for dinner?"

"I'm not sure." I rubbed the lip gloss from his mouth with my thumb. "I have a meeting at the school this evening, but I don't know how long it'll take."

"I'll give you a call later, and we'll see where we're at." He dropped another kiss on my lips. "Sorry I undid your cleanup. Couldn't help myself."

I chuckled as he ducked out the door and into the hallway. Waiting until I heard his footsteps fading, I turned to see Max grinning at me. "Was I mistaken, or did I hear you gasp when Jason asked me for sugar?"

"You weren't mistaken—I gasped." She raised and lowered one slim shoulder.

"Why? I didn't expect you—especially after the way you championed my dating Jason—to take offense at a teensy bit of kissing in the workplace."

"Darling, in my day, sugar meant money. And I was gonna be sorely disappointed in your young man if he came by here to ask you for money. But that kiss was dreamy." She jerked her head toward the reception area. "Would you mind bringing the tablet in here so we can work together?"

"No, of course not." I retrieved the tablet and placed it on the edge of the table where Max could sit and read or whatever she wanted to do.

Ruby Mills called and told me she loved the dress. "Sew 'er up, Amanda."

Laughing, I said, "I sure will. You can come in for the first fitting on Saturday, if that works."

"Works for me. See you then."

After ending the call, I walked over to the shelf and got a bolt of black crepe de chine. Looking over my design, Max said, "I like this."

"Thanks. What're you working on today?"

"I started reading that nonfiction book on the Great Depression I asked you to download for me, but it was too darned depressing." She sighed. "I'm sorry. Can you send it back?"

"Sure, no problem. What would you prefer to read?" I asked. "Or would you rather watch something?"

"I could go for something funny. Have you got anything?"

I smiled. "I think I've got just the thing."

Listening to Max's howls of laughter as she watched *I Love Lucy*, I cut out the bodice for Ruby's dress.

Grandpa Dave called hello as he came through the door leading to the reception area.

"Back here!"

"That's what I figured." He came into the atelier and kissed my cheek. "I could hear Max laughing all the way out in the hall. What's so funny?"

"It's the first episode of *I Love Lucy*," I said.

"Where she thinks Ricky is trying to kill her?" He went to look at the tablet and chuckled. "Yeah, that's a good one."

Jazzy got out of her bed and wound around Grandpa's ankles.

Laying the bodice aside, I spread out the fabric for the skirt. "What are you doing in town?"

"I'm here to see Ford, but I wanted to stop in and see my favorite girls first," he said.

"A silver fox with a silver tongue," Max said, putting the back of her hand to her forehead as if she were about to faint.

"Looking for anything in particular?" I asked.

"Yeah—help with this library set I'm trying to figure out. I'm hoping Ford can provide some insights."

"Amanda told me you and she might be able to use computers to let me see some of the work taking place for the play." Max clasped her hands together and placed them under her chin. "She said maybe I could see some of the practices."

"I've never done a live feed." Grandpa turned to me. "Have you?"

"No, but I don't think it'll be that hard to figure out." I pinned the pattern to the fabric.

"I'll go on up and talk with Ford," he said. "See you two in a bit."

Hearing the door open in the reception area again, I took the pin cushion from my wrist and went to see who was there. It was a stylish woman who appeared to be in her mid-forties.

"Hello, and welcome to Designs on You. I'm Amanda. Is there anything in particular I could help you with?"

"Yes. I'm looking for a dress for my daughter to wear to the homecoming tomorrow night. I know it's last minute. I meant to come by ages ago, but I kept getting busy with one thing and another." She waved her hand. "You know how it is."

"Of course. I still have a wide selection of ready-to-wear styles fitting the homecoming theme." I showed the woman where the *pret a porter* dresses were hanging.

As the woman was looking through the dresses on the rack, I said, "I've been asked to help with costumes for *Beauty and the Beast.* Will your daughter be participating in the play?"

She froze. "No, she most certainly will not. And, if you know what's good for you, you won't turn your back on Sandra Kelly."

Chapter Five

"Gee," Max said, after the customer left. "Wonder what that was all about?"

"I don't know." I shrugged. "Sandra seems perfectly nice to me."

"True. But, then, she wants something from you. You don't usually show your true colors around someone when you want them to think you're the elephant's eyebrows." She inclined her head. "At least, not until you get what you want from them."

"I'll keep my eyes and ears open," I promised. "But, like her or not, this is decent pay and excellent exposure for Designs on You."

Grandpa breezed in through the door to the atelier.

"How did the meeting with Ford go?" Max asked. "Did he give you any helpful pointers?"

"Even better." He grinned. "He's offered to help me build the library set." Scooping up Jazzy, who'd come to wind around his ankles, he said, "If you'll get her carrier, I'll take her home with me."

"I wish you could take me home with you. I'd love to see where you live...and where Amanda lives." She gave a dramatic sigh. "This place hasn't changed much over the years."

"I promise when we get the live streaming figured out, you'll see lots of places." I got the carrier for Grandpa.

She chuckled. "That'd be swell. But, nuts, you two have given me so much already. I'm ashamed of myself for wanting more."

"Never stop dreaming." Grandpa put Jazzy into her carrier. "And don't ever stop wanting more out of life. As soon as you do, you might as well be—"

Neither Max nor I could hold back the laughter that bubbled up within us. And when we laughed, Grandpa got over his faux pas and let out a guffaw of his own.

"I'm flattered you don't think of me as dead, Dave," Max said. "Thanks to you and Amanda, I'm more alive now than I have been in decades."

Max had slipped away, and I had just finished cutting out Ruby Miller's dress pattern when a customer came into Designs on You. I called into the reception area that I'd be right out, and then I folded up the pattern and set it aside.

Walking out of the atelier, I could remember seeing the woman before, but I couldn't quite place her. Had she browsed in the shop before, or did I know her from the grocery store or the bank? It was hard to say in a small town like Abingdon.

"Hi." The woman turned from looking at the Renaissance dress on the mannequin and gave me a bright smile. "This is gorgeous."

"Thank you," I said. "Are you looking for a costume?"

"Goodness, no. I just wanted to stop in and get a proper look at your designs while my son is still at school."

Now I recognized her. "Do you have a little boy named Joey?"

She laughed. "Yes. And he has two ferrets named Biscuit and Gravy that got out of his backpack and ran all over this place. Am I still welcome at Shops on Main?"

"Of course, you are! And so is Joey. He really livened things up that day."

"He livens things up every day." She stuck out her hand. "I'm Sarah Conrad."

"Amanda Tucker." I shook her hand. "It's nice to actually meet you. What a coincidence you stopped in today. I'm helping out with the costumes for the Winter Garden High School play, and I learned that Joey is going to be Chip, the teacup."

"Yeah." Her smile faded. "I'm more than a little nervous about Joey being in a high school production."

"I'm sure he'll do a great job," I said. "Ms. Kelly wouldn't have cast him if she didn't think so too."

Sarah's eyes widened. "I hope she knows what she's doing. Abingdon High did that play last year, and one of the seniors played Chip. He was on some sort of little rolling stool the whole time, so he'd be shorter than the rest of the cast."

"Do you know Ms. Kelly well?" I asked.

"Not really, but all her students—my niece Stephanie included—seem to think the world of her." She wandered over to the ready-to-wear clothes and picked out a royal blue sheath with a matching chiffon wrap. Holding the dress beneath her chin before the full-length mirror, she asked. "What do you think?"

"I think you'd look gorgeous in that. It really brings out your eyes." I indicated the Oriental screen that hid the fitting area. "Why don't you try it on?"

She bit her lip and then grinned. "Okay."

Moments later, she stood before the three-way mirror as I pinned up the hem. The dress had been a little too long for Sarah's petite frame.

"Would you like to wait while I hem this?" I asked. "It'll only take a few minutes."

"I can't. I have to get to that interminable car rider line. Will it be all right if I drop in and pick it up tomorrow?"

"Sure." I glanced up at her before taking another pin from the pin cushion on my wrist. "Or I could bring it to the practice tonight."

"Oh, that's all right. Joey won't be there. They want to get the middle schoolers in and go through their stuff tonight. They're not bringing Joey in until Monday." She gave a short laugh. "That should give Ms. Kelly one last weekend of sanity."

Grandpa and I strolled down the hallway toward the high school's auditorium. Homecoming posters and streamers in blue and gold decorated both sides above the lockers.

Zoe was standing at the stage door waiting for us. "There's a big dude with bushy hair waiting for you guys. I think he said his name was Ford."

Nodding, Grandpa confirmed that the imposing man was indeed Ford, a bookshop owner, who would be helping with the library set.

"Cool," Zoe said. "He freaked some of the kids out a little, but when he spouted off some Shakespeare, I figured he was all right."

As we walked backstage, I overheard some girls talking. Their voices were, appropriately enough, in stage whispers.

"She's probably somewhere playing kissy-face with Mr. Talbot," one said.

Two of the girls giggled, but another screwed up her face. "I think it's disgusting," she said. "My parents broke up over an affair, and it's horrible. I still haven't hundred percent forgiven my mom."

The third girl in the group rolled her eyes and tossed her long blonde hair over her shoulder. "Don't be so freakin' dramatic, Alyssa. There's scientific proof that monogamy is a fallacy anyway."

The "disgusted" girl scoffed. "You're only saying that because you don't have a boyfriend right now."

"Knock it off," Zoe told them. "We're not here to gossip about Ms. Kelly. We're here to work on our senior play."

Two of the girls lowered their eyes and nodded, but the hair-tosser merely flipped her hair again and walked away.

Waiting until the girls were out of earshot, I asked Zoe, "Ms. Kelly isn't here yet?"

She shook her head and avoided my eyes. "I know what we're supposed to be doing, though. We can handle it."

Grandpa spotted Ford, and the two of them—along with the other set volunteers—took their supplies out into the hallway to work without disturbing the actors. Zoe enlisted the help of the middle school teacher—a man who appeared to be in his early- to mid-thirties named Mr. Clark—to help corral the extras from the middle school drama club so she could give them some instructions. Kristen decided to practice her opening song with the pianist. And I gathered up the volunteer seamstresses to sit with me in the back of the auditorium with a list of the performers and the costumes we'd need.

An hour later, Sandra Kelly still hadn't made an appearance, and no one had heard from her either. Zoe pulled me aside and said she'd tried to call Ms. Kelly but hadn't got an answer.

"I'm getting worried. Do you think she could be sick or something?" she asked.

"Let's hope not." I assured Zoe I'd call around and see if I could track Ms. Kelly down. My first thought was to call Connie.

"Hello." Connie's soft voice sounded as peaceful and content as ever.

"Connie, hi, this is Amanda. I'm calling from Winter Garden High. Sandra Kelly hasn't shown up for play practice, and she isn't answering her phone. Do you know how I might reach her?"

"I just closed up shop and was heading for the school myself. I'll go by her house and see if she's there."

"Thank you." I ended the call and told Zoe that someone was driving by Ms. Kelly's house to make sure everything was all right.

I went back to my group and handed out assignments for some of the easier costumes.

"Anytime you'd like to call me stop or by Designs on You, I'll be happy to help you." That's what I was cheerily saying when my phone rang. I looked at the screen and saw that the caller was Connie. "Excuse me please. This is Connie—she offered to go by Ms. Kelly's house and check on her."

The women nodded and went back to talking among themselves about the costumes. I stepped out into the hallway and answered Connie's call.

"Hi, Connie."

"She's d-dead. Sandy's...dead."

"What?" Maybe I hadn't heard her correctly. But, then, she'd spoken pretty clearly, even though her voice was no longer soft and peaceful but shaky and terrified. "Connie, where are you? I'll come get you."

"I-I called the police, and they're here now. And they...they had me call Will." She sniffled. "He's c-coming to g-get me."

"How can I help?" I asked. "What can I do?"

"C-can you bring Marielle home? Please?"

"Of course." I saw Zoe poke her head out into the hallway, and I turned away. I didn't want to burden her with this yet. She was a kid. And, yet, I instinctively knew that she'd handle the matter with more discretion than many of the adults. Plus, I didn't want her to be blindsided by rumors tomorrow at school. I turned back and motioned for her to join me. "We'll be there soon, Connie."

"What's up?" Zoe asked. "Is Ms. Kelly sick or something?"

I took a deep breath. "She's dead."

Chapter Six

After I'd rounded up the staff and explained the situation, Mrs. Berry—another English teacher helping out with the production—made the announcement that play rehearsal was ending early due to unforeseen circumstances. There were a lot of whispers, and a couple of the students asked why, but Mrs. Berry remained firm and kept everything under control. The older woman looked like she had a backbone made of steel, and I imagined she'd seen a lot in her time at Winter Garden High. She was no pushover, and she certainly wasn't going to say or do anything that would add fuel to the fiery gossip in which the students were already engaging.

A few of the mutterings I heard were: Has Ms. Kelly ran off and deserted us too? Would the play still happen? Had Ms. Kelly been caught with Mr. Talbot, and had both of them been fired? It would serve them right. But it wouldn't be fair to the students. No one seemed to suspect the truth. I admired

Zoe's self-restraint, but I knew she had to be worried.

Unable to find Marielle in the crowd, I took the microphone and announced that I'd be taking her home. She quickly and quietly made her way to the front of the auditorium. She was a sweet kid—shy, smart, and soft spoken. I thought she and Zoe would be good foils for each other and wondered if they were friends.

Grandpa Dave and Ford were reluctant to quit working on their balcony, but I reminded them that they were about to get locked in the school overnight. Neither man wanted to be stuck for hours with nothing more than a hard floor and cafeteria food, so they agreed to come back tomorrow.

"So, what's up?" Ford asked. "We'd barely gotten started."

I gave the crowd a pointed stare. "I'll explain later."

Ford nodded, scowled, and scanned the students leaving the auditorium. "Wasn't a bomb threat, was it?"

"No," I said. "It definitely wasn't that."

I spoke with Mrs. Berry and explained that Connie had asked me to take Marielle home. "Is there anything you need me to help you with before I go?"

Mrs. Berry shook her head. "I just can't quite get my head around this terrible business. I'm not sure what the school will want to do about the play now, but I'll let you know."

"All right. Thank you." As I went to collect Marielle and Grandpa Dave, I wondered about the fact that Mrs. Berry seemed to be more upset about the play than she did the fact that Ms. Kelly was dead. Of course, she was probably in shock. I knew I was. The other staff members appeared to be as well.

Upon telling Ford I'd see him tomorrow at work—and trusting him to understand that meant I'd explain the situation to him then—Grandpa Dave, Marielle, and I left the school. I looked for Zoe but didn't see her.

At least, I didn't see her inside the school. I saw her walking along the shoulder a few hundred yards down the road. I slowed the car and put down my window.

"Zoe, get in here!" I called.

The girl stopped. "I'm all right."

"Please. I need to know you're going to get home safely."

"I will. I do this all the time," Zoe said.

"Will you humor me—just this once?" I asked.

She blew out a breath, looked to make sure no cars were coming in the other direction, and then crossed the road and got into the backseat with Marielle. "Hey."

"Hey," Marielle said.

I put the window up and resumed driving. Glancing into the rearview mirror, I asked Zoe, "Where do you live?"

"Go to the end of this road and take a right."

"Okay." Both Marielle and Zoe looked uncomfortable. I decided to try to break the ice. "Zoe, Marielle, do you guys know each other?"

"We had French together last year," Marielle said.

"Yeah." Zoe gave a bark of laughter. "Marielle speaks it like she was born there. I can barely say parlez vous."

"That's not true. You did...fine." Marielle had her mother's gentle, encouraging nature.

"Fine. Right." Zoe laughed again. "Eh, I passed. That's all I cared about."

I'd turned right at the end of the road as Zoe had instructed. We were on a street with beautiful houses with manicured lawns. While it wasn't my intention to be judgmental, Zoe didn't look as if she fit in with the neighborhood.

"You can just let me out here, Amanda," she said. "I'll walk the rest of the way. The dog freaks out whenever a strange car pulls into our driveway."

"Are you sure?" I asked.

"Yep. See you later." She opened the car door. "Hopefully." She got out and walked up the street.

I turned around in the cul-de-sac, and Zoe waved to us from in front of a brick home with white columns on the porch. I waved back and drove on down the street. In my rearview mirror, I saw her jog across the street and through the backyards of the homes.

Where was she going? And why hadn't she been honest with me about where she lived?

I considered going back, but I felt as if I'd already made things worse by offering her a ride home in the first place. Had I left her alone, would she have been safer than she would have been prowling around in people's backyards in the evening?

Will and Connie sat on the sofa. Will had a blanket and both arms around his wife, and she had her head resting on his shoulder.

"Mom, what happened?" Marielle hurried over and sank to the floor in front of her parents. "Where's Charlie?"

"He's upstairs playing video games." Will looked at me. "What does she know?"

"Nothing," I said. "I thought it best for you and Connie to talk with her."

He nodded. "Right. Thanks."

"What's going on?" Marielle asked.

"Ms. Kelly is dead," Connie said quietly. "I went to her house to check on her since she hadn't shown up at play practice. And I...I found her."

"Wow. That's awful." Marielle took her mother's hand. "Do you know what happened?"

Connie slowly shook her head. "I don't. I don't know."

Thinking it best if we left, I said goodbye and asked Connie to let me know if she needed anything.

In the car, Grandpa Dave asked, "What do you think did happen? Heart attack, maybe? Ms. Kelly appeared to be in good health, but she definitely had one of those Type A personalities."

"True. But she seemed fine earlier today." I shuddered. "That's so scary—someone can be laughing and fine at lunch and then dead by dinner."

"What about the play? Do you think the show will still go on?" he asked.

"I don't know." I frowned slightly. "Some of the staff members—and, particularly the parents—seemed more concerned about the status of the play than they did the fact that Sandra Kelly was dead."

"Well, it's the senior play—the last time many of the students will get to participate in something like that." He shrugged. "And I do believe participation in school productions looks good on college applications."

"True. I also got the impression that Sandra had a polarizing personality," I said. "People seemed to have loved her or hated her."

"I got that feeling too. No one was wishy-washy when it came to describing how they felt about the woman," Grandpa Dave said. "And what about Zoe?"

I glanced at him. "You mean the way she lied to us about where she lived?"

"Exactly. I thought you'd caught that too, but I wasn't certain."

"I started to go back." I blew out a breath. "But I was afraid that might make things even worse. Do you think she did it because she's ashamed of where she lives?"

"More than likely." He paused. "Especially since she probably thinks Marielle has a nice house—which, of course, she does."

"Yeah, but still... I think there's more to it than that. Sandra told me at lunch today that she thinks Zoe is sad—that she sometimes volunteers for projects so she doesn't have to go home after school."

"I hope that's not the case, Pup. But, even if it is, there's not much you can do about it."

"I know," I said. "Unless someone is being mean to her. That's something I can and will do something about."

He laughed softly. "You're putting the cart before the horse. You don't even know Zoe does have an unhappy homelife. You're merely guessing and going on the word of someone else—someone who can't expand on the subject now."

"I suppose I'll simply have to find out some other way." I didn't know how I'd do that, but I would. I couldn't stand the thought of anyone mistreating that extraordinary girl

Chapter Seven

I was happy to get inside my warm, safe home. Of course, Sandra Kelly had been inside her presumably warm, safe home when she died. What on earth had happened to her? Had it been a heart attack, as Grandpa Dave suggested? That seemed to be the most likely. For her to be so vibrant and alive at midday and then dead that evening—barring an accident of some sort—it had to be an emergency so sudden she didn't even have the opportunity to call 911.

And poor Connie! She was so traumatized. I could only imagine how horrified she must've been at finding Sandra dead. Would she be able to open Delightful Home tomorrow? If not, I should take some food over—maybe a pizza. I felt confident the kids would like that.

To get my mind off Sandra, Connie, the play, and Zoe, I opened my laptop and got to work on my project for Max. Finding Dot was easier than I'd expected once I keyed her information into a popular genealogy site. Dorothy Ann Englebright had married Joseph Hall at age twenty-one. She'd given birth to a daughter named Maxine in 1937 and a son named Dwight in 1939.

Maxine. I blinked back tears. Dot had named her daughter after Max. I could hardly wait to tell her.

My doorbell rang. I closed the laptop and placed it on the coffee table before going to the door. Peeping out the window, I was happy to see Jason standing on the porch. He had a white dog in his arms.

Flinging open the door, I exclaimed, "This must be Rascal!"

The dog began wriggling with excitement.

"It is," Jason said, as he stepped into the living room. "I don't want to put him down until we know he won't freak out Jazzy."

"Go ahead." I reached out to let the dog sniff and lick my hand before petting him. "She's met dogs before. I think she'll be fine."

I closed the door, sat on the sofa, and patted the cushion beside me. I'd intended for Jason to take the seat, but Rascal beat him to it and began covering my face in doggie kisses.

Laughing, I asked, "Is he always like this?"

"Pretty much." Jason plucked Rascal off the sofa, sat beside me, and held the dog on his lap. That didn't last for long. The rowdy pup squirmed out of his arms and was back to kissing me in no time. "He'll calm down in a minute."

"I know," I said. Actually, I didn't know. But as I stroked Rascal's wiry fur and talked to him, the newness of the situation wore off enough that he stretched out across my lap. He still demanded my attention, but he wasn't as insistent about it as he was before.

"I hope you don't mind my dropping in on you like this, but I was driving by and saw your lights on and decided to take a chance."

"I'm glad you did. Play practice was cut short because of Sandra Kelly's death."

His jaw dropped. "What happened?"

"I have no idea. Everyone else was there getting ready to rehearse, and people were starting to get concerned about Sandra," I said. "I called Connie to see if she knew what I should do, and she offered to stop by Sandra's house on the way to the school."

"Aw, man, Connie found her? That's terrible."

"It is. Connie called the ambulance and the police—or else, she called the ambulance, and paramedics called police, I'm fuzzy on the details."

"And you have no clue as to cause of death?" he asked.

Shaking my head, I said, "Grandpa Dave and I are guessing heart attack because that seems to be the most likely scenario, but we're only making assumptions—which we really shouldn't do. Did you know Sandra?"

"Not well. I'm acquainted with her from taking portraits at the school, but that's the extent of my association with her." He frowned slightly. "You know, I think she might've been a client of Carla's. I should let her know about Sandra's death."

"You should." I was relieved that he didn't immediately take out his phone.

Jazzy finally got up the nerve to imperiously investigate Rascal. Tail held high and twitching, the cat hopped onto the arm of the sofa. Rascal stilled. As he inspected this new creature, his tail began to slowly wag. He stood up on my lap and stretched his neck out. Jazzy leaned in and sniffed the dog's head. Rascal's tail wagged faster, and he licked Jazzy's face. She batted him on the nose, but kept her claws retracted. Rascal leapt onto the floor before posing front paws out and butt in the air—the universal dog sign for let's play. When Jazzy didn't immediately join him, the dog ran around the coffee table before stopping in front of her and slapping the floor with his front paws. On his next lap around, Jazzy jumped down and gave chase. They ran through the living room and into the kitchen. When they came back, Rascal was trailing Jazzy.

They played like that for the better part of twenty minutes before lying down near each other and going to sleep.

"I believe they've got the right idea," Jason said.

"I think you're right." I nestled against him, and we watched TV.

When I arrived at Designs on You on Friday morning, I didn't see Max. I was kinda glad. I had a lot to tell her, but I wanted to check on Connie first. I heard her minivan pull into the parking lot not long after I'd arrived, I decided to take her a cup of Kava tea.

Ford was in the kitchen. "What happened last night?"

"Sandra Kelly is dead," I answered.

"Who's she?"

It hadn't occurred to me that Ford hadn't met Sandra yet. "She's a teacher at Winter Garden High and the director of the play." I filled a mug with water. "I'm making Connie a cup of tea. She's the one who found Sandra's body."

"Woah. That's intense." Before I could say anything more, Ford took his coffee and strode down the hall.

I knew he was going to see Connie, and I hurried to catch up with him. I didn't want her to think I was talking about her to Ford—which, of course, I had been, but it wasn't like that. I don't know—maybe it was like that, but I wanted to be there to explain my position when he opened his big mouth to Connie.

"Connie," Ford was saying as I followed him into Delightful Home. He opened his arms and engulfed the woman in a hug. "Are you all right? Amanda told me what happened."

"I'm sorry, Connie," I said quickly, hoping she could hear me through Ford's fortress of muscle and cotton. "Ford was helping Grandpa Dave with the set design last night and wondered why we'd called off practice."

"It's okay." She stepped out of Ford's embrace and walked over to the stool that sat behind the counter. "It was a rough evening, but I'm all right."

"I was making you some Kava tea," I said.

She held up a mug. "Way ahead of you, hon. But I appreciate the thought."

"You wanna talk about what happened?" Ford asked. "If you don't, we'll respect your privacy." He leaned across the counter.

I couldn't fault the man. I, too, wanted to know what the heck had happened after Connie volunteered to check on Sandra Kelly yesterday evening.

"There's not a lot to tell," she began in her soft voice. "I stopped by Sandy's house and knocked, but she didn't answer. Since she hadn't been answering her phone, the fact that she didn't come to the door worried me, especially since her car was in the driveway. I turned the knob, and since the door was unlocked, I opened it and called to Sandy from the doorway."

I noticed Max in the corner near Connie. She met my eyes but said nothing.

"When she didn't answer, I went inside. I didn't even think about the possibility of getting in trouble—"

"You didn't, did you?" Ford interrupted her.

"No. The police were very nice to me." Connie gave him a sad smile that faded as she continued her narrative. "Although they did ask me a lot of questions."

"Like what?" he asked.

She gave a slight shrug. "They asked me if I'd noticed any glasses or plates Sandy might've been using. But since Sandy was in the living room, I didn't go anywhere except that room, and there weren't any dishes in there."

"The coppers must think she was poisoned," Max murmured.

Connie shuddered. "She looked so awful lying there on the floor. Her...her head was a mess—clumps of hair had fallen out, and her scalp was bleeding."

"Had she been hit on the head?" I asked.

"I don't know," Connie said. "But I don't think so. The wounds looked more like abrasions than cuts." She squinted into the distance. "And the room smelled like pineapple."

"So she had been eating?" Ford asked.

"No. I think maybe it was room freshener or something." She wrinkled her nose. "It just smelled rank to me. I don't think I'll ever be able to eat pineapple again."

Chapter Eight

Back inside the atelier at Designs on You with the door shut, I gave Max an abbreviated version of what had occurred the night before. She'd already determined from the conversation in Delightful Home that Connie had found Sandra Kelly dead yesterday evening, so I filled her in on the events leading up to the discovery.

"What a rotten thing to have happen to a poor little bunny like Connie," Max said. "Had I found Sandra Kelly, I'd have cased the joint to see if I could figure out what did her in." She shrugged. "Of course, I've been dead a long time, and I'm kinda jaded."

"Kinda," I agreed. "We didn't announce to the kids that Sandra was dead, but we quietly told the parents and staff. Their reactions fell into two camps—those who were sorry about Sandra's misfortune and those who were merely concerned about the play going forward without her."

"Well, I can understand that. If they didn't know Sandra very well, their minds would be on their kiddos and how disappointed they'd be if the play was canceled."

"True, but some who did know Sandra didn't seem terribly broken up about her death." I walked over to the rack and took down Ruby Mills' dress. All I needed to do was put the zipper in before calling Ruby to come in for her fitting. "Something else weird happened last night. Remember Zoe, the girl I told you about?"

"The stage manager?" Max asked.

"Yeah. I insisted she let me take her home, and she lied to me about where she lived. I saw her leave the porch and hurry across the street as I was driving away."

She waggled her fingers at Jazzy, who'd come to sit near her. "Maybe the gal's just private—didn't want you knowing her beeswax."

"That, or she's ashamed of where she lives," I said.

"True." Shaking her head, she said, "I don't know much about today's youth. I imagine you should keep mum about what you saw—if she wants you to know something, she'll tell you."

"I guess." I chose a black zipper and sat at the sewing machine with the dress. "But I'm keeping an eye on her." I began basting the zipper to the dress. "Jason stopped by my house last night—which was nice—but when I told him about Sandra Kelly, he said he thought she'd been a client of Carla's."

"Carla? Miz Boom-Chicka-Boom? Keep-Your-Piehole-Closed-Frank? That Carla?"

Laughing at Max's description, I said, "Yep. The very one. Jason said he should call her."

Max growled. "He didn't, did he?"

"Not while he was with me." I finished basting the zipper as Max ranted on about Carla, and then I looked up. "I can't believe that with all the excitement I forgot to tell you—I found Dot."

"What?" She sank slowly onto the worktable like a deflating balloon.

"In 1935, Dot married Joseph Hall. She gave birth to a daughter in 1937 and a son in 1939." I grinned. "Want to know their names?"

She nodded.

"Maxine and Dwight," I said.

With tears in her eyes, she whispered, "She named her daughter after me."

"Of course, she did!" I'd never wanted to hug Max more than I did in that moment.

It took her a moment to find her voice again, but when she did, she took full advantage of it. "What else did you learn? When did Dot die? What did Joseph do for a living? What happened to Maxine and Dwight?"

"I don't know. I'd only found out what I did when Jason arrived."

"But you'll find out, right?" she asked.

"Of course, I will."

"Thank you." She gave me a shaky smile. "I need a few minutes." With that, she was gone.

About an hour later, Trish Oakes brought another possible new vendor by for me to meet. This woman had reddish gold hair, appeared to be in her mid-forties, and had a ready smile.

"Amanda Tucker, I'd like you to meet Barbara Shipley," Ms. Oakes said.

"Please call me Barb." The newcomer held out her hand for me to shake. She had a warm, firm grip.

"Barb, it's a pleasure to meet you," I said. "What do you do?"

"I'm an artist. I paint pet portraits." She glanced around the atelier and caught sight of Jazzy in her bed. "Oh, wow. What a beauty!" She went closer, and Jazzy looked up at her warily. "What's her name?"

"It's Jasmine, but I call her Jazzy most of the time," I said.

Barb tsked. "Oh, Jazzy isn't dignified enough for you, is it, princess?" She turned back to me. "May I paint her?"

"No, thanks," Max piped up.

I stiffened, trying to ready myself for whatever the ghostly fashionista might say next.

"We like her the color she is."

Barely able to suppress a giggle, I said, "Thank you, Barb. I'll consider it."

"But you must let me paint her." Barb left Jazzy long enough to return to me and plead her case. "She's absolutely magical. Watch her—it's as if she's looking at something right now that no one else can see."

Max patted her hair and winked.

"I'll give it some thought." Actually, if Barb could somehow paint Jazzy looking up at Max—and include Max in the portrait—that's something I wouldn't mind paying a pretty penny for.

"Come, Ms. Shipley," Ms. Oakes said. "Let me introduce you to the Petermans. They're a lovely couple."

Hands on her hips, Max said, "She said that as if she were implying that we aren't a lovely couple. And I, for one, think we're the elephant's eyebrows."

"So do I." I smiled. "Wonder what Barb Shipley and Teddy Bare would make of each other—particularly, each other's work?"

"I don't know." She rested her chin on her index finger. "Somehow, I don't think she'd find his happy taxidermy critters all that magical."

After I called Ruby Mills and scheduled her fitting for that afternoon, Max said, "I haven't noticed anyone coming in yet about homecoming dresses. It's still early in the day, of course, but I'm wondering if the school canceled it because of Ms. Kelly's death."

"I seriously doubt that. Only snow can cancel a high school football game, and I imagine it would take a blizzard to stand between a homecoming queen and her crown."

"Especially if our very own Princess Kristen is vying for the crown." Max mimed putting on a crown, framing her face with her hands, and giving a smug shrug.

Following a quick rap on the atelier door, Jason popped his head into the room. "Hey, there. I stopped by to pick up some proofs, but I wanted to say hi and see if you're going to be here at lunchtime."

"I will." I got up from the sewing machine and went over to kiss him hello.

"I spoke with Carla this morning. She was upset to hear about Sandra Kelly and said she might stop by here at lunchtime," he said. "Since you're going to be here, I thought I'd bring back some lunch, and we could all eat in the kitchen. How does that sound?"

"Like a nightmare!" Max yelled. "Do you truly think Amanda and I want to take our midday refreshment with some floozy that's trying to horn in on your relationship?"

"That sounds great," I said.

After another peck on the lips, Jason left. Once I'd heard his footsteps echoing down the hall, I turned to Max. "Our midday refreshment?"

Pursing her lips, Max said, "Just because I can't eat, doesn't mean I'm not refreshed by our midday break."

"You don't have to be there, you know."

She flattened her palm against her chest. "Ha! I wouldn't miss it for all the gold in King Tut's tomb."

Great. I didn't know if I could handle Max and Carla at the same time. Lunch wouldn't be boring—that was for sure.

There was a busy spell around ten-thirty that morning. A couple of women came by for last-minute dresses for their daughters for the homecoming dance, and then a younger woman came in and bought the Renaissance dress right off the mannequin for an upcoming cosplay event.

I was redressing the mannequin when I got a phone call. Using the cheery, professional tone I used for unknown numbers, I answered, "Good morning! Thank you for calling Designs on You. This is Amanda—how may I help you?"

"Ms. Tucker, this is Sylvia Berry. I'm calling to inform you that *Beauty and the Beast* will go forward."

Mrs. Berry's voice was as clipped and dry as I'd remembered. I wasn't surprised she didn't engage in any small talk but got straight to the point.

"I've spoken with the principal, who has been getting calls from parents all morning, and the board has decided to proceed with the production," she continued. "It was mentioned that some sort of memorial to Sandra Kelly could be made in the program, but that's something for others to decide and deal with—not I. My concern is the production itself. May we still rely on you, Ms. Tucker?"

"Absolutely," I said.

"Very well. Since play practice was cut short yesterday evening, there will be a makeup rehearsal on Saturday afternoon. Will you be in attendance?"

"I'll be there," I said. "I'll look forward to seeing you then."

"Yes. Goodbye."

I grinned and shook my head as I ended the call. Yes? Who says that? Couldn't she have said, 'I'll look forward to seeing you too'? Then again, maybe she didn't.

I considered going across the hall to tell Connie that the play was going forward, but when I opened the reception room door, I saw that she had customers in her shop. I closed the door and returned to the atelier. I supposed Marielle would let her mother know about the play. Plus, I didn't want to keep reminding Connie about Sandra Kelly's death.

Chapter Nine

Jason texted me shortly after noon to let me know he was on his way with subs and chips. I asked if there was enough to include Connie, and he sent back a reply that he'd gotten extra in case any of the other vendors wanted to join us.

"That's really thoughtful of him," I said aloud.

Max interrupted my musing with, "Fiddle sticks!"

"What is it?" I hadn't even known she was back from wherever she'd disappeared to.

"They're getting out of the car," she said, hands anchored on her slim hips.

"Who?"

"Jason and that tomato!"

"Carla?" I asked. "I hadn't realized she was with him."

"Oh, she's with him, all right. And wait until you see what she's wearing." Raising her fists and screwing up her face, Max said, "I'm gonna haunt her." She warmed to the thought. "I'm going to haunt the tee-total dickens out of that Jezebel so that she never wants to come here again."

"How?" Did I really want to know the answer to that? Yes. "What are you planning to do?"

"I'm not sure. But I'll figure something out." She punctuated her words with a strong nod. "Wait and see if I don't."

Before I could try to dissuade her—or decide if I wanted to, for that matter—Jason stepped into the atelier and said, "Lunch is here!"

I pushed back from my chair and stood, thinking Max couldn't do much harm. It wasn't as if Carla could see her. And Max couldn't touch the woman. I figured my biggest worry would be restraining my-self from laughing at any of her antics.

Stepping into the kitchen, I saw what Max meant about Carla's outfit. She wore a cropped white sweater that fell off her shoulders and tight black capri pants. She looked lovely, but I could certainly imagine her making Frank lose his gum again should he be chewing any today.

"I'm going to see if anyone wants to have lunch with us," Jason said, giving me a kiss on the cheek before he left me alone with Carla in the kitchen.

"Nice to see you again, Carla. Jason said he thought Sandra Kelly was a client of yours."

"Yes, she was. I think Jason is absolutely precious to remember that after all these years. And he was an angel to come pick me up to have lunch with all of you so I wouldn't have to be alone dwelling on her death all day."

What? The woman doesn't have clients? Or did she cancel them for the day? "You and Sandra were close then?"

She nodded. "Sandy had been seeing me for years for her sciatica. She was sweet—paid when services were rendered and always added a generous tip."

That didn't sound like a friend to me—more like a loyal client. I tried again. "The people I've spoken with who knew her from school either loved her or hated her. There didn't seem to be much middle ground where she was concerned."

"Lump me into the first category," Carla said.

I was only half startled when a man's scream emanated from the atelier, but I had to lower my head and turn away slightly to hide my grin.

Carla gasped. "What was that?"

Not knowing what else to do, I played dumb. "What?"

"That noise. You have to have heard it."

"Well...um...whatever it was, it wasn't me." I went to the refrigerator and opened the door.

The next thing I heard was a man saying, "Go on now—git! Git on up out of here!"

Pressing my lips together, I surveyed the contents of the fridge for a few seconds to hide my face from Carla. "How are you doing that?" I whispered to Max.

"You had to have heard that!" Carla was obviously getting flustered.

"I've been playing with that video movie thingy," Max said, appearing atop the fridge. "It has everything you could possibly want on there. Fascinating." With a wink, she disappeared.

That wink said she wasn't done—not by a longshot.

"Hello." It was Connie.

"Hi," I said. "Would either of you care for a soft drink?"

"I have tea," Connie said, "but thank you."

"Jason got me a bottle of water from the restaurant where he got the sandwiches," Carla said, removing the bottle from her purse.

"Does your joining us mean you're leasing the space upstairs?" Connie asked.

"No. It would be too hard from some of my clients to navigate the stairs. Too bad this place doesn't have an elevator." She pulled out a chair and sat. "It stinks that this place is stuck in the past, right? Jason and I have been good friends for ages, and I'd have enjoyed working right across the hall from him."

And that was when Frank Sinatra—or a reasonable facsimile thereof—belted out from the depths of Carla's purse that the lady was a tramp.

I burst out laughing. There'd been no way to repress that one. Thankfully, Connie laughed too. Max, of course, had resumed her seat atop the refrigerator and was kicking her legs and clapping.

"Is that your phone's ringtone?" Connie asked Carla.

Jason and Ford entered the kitchen as Carla said, "No, it most certainly is not."

"What's going on?" Jason looked from Carla to me.

"We heard Frank Sinatra singing and thought it might be Carla's phone," I said.

Carla ran a well-manicured hand over her forehead. "I've been hearing strange things ever since I got here." She narrowed her eyes at me. "And I've been with you the whole time. Are you pranking me?"

"No. Even if I was a gifted ventriloquist, I could never hope to sound so much like Frank Sinatra. It was as if Old Blue Eyes himself were right here in this kitchen." My eyes flew to Max. "He wasn't, was he?" Chuckling to cover for my blunder, I looked at Jason. "I mean, you and I have spoken about the possibility of ghosts inhabiting these old buildings."

"That's nonsense," Jason said. He turned to Carla. "I believe you're on edge over the death of your client."

"That wasn't the disembodied voice of a ghost," Connie said. "I'm positive it came from your purse, Carla. Maybe you bumped your mp3 player or something." She sat beside Carla. "I'm sorry you've suffered a recent loss."

"Her client was Sandra Kelly," I said.

"Really? What a coincidence," Connie said. "Sandy and I were friends in college, lost touch, and then reconnected when my daughter became interested in drama and we saw last year's production of Dracula at Winter Garden High."

"Connie found Ms. Kelly's body last night," Ford blurted out as he sat on the other side of Carla.

That's our sensitive Ford.

Did I imagine Carla's flash of irritation at Ford's taking the empty seat? Had she hoped Jason would sit there? If so, she hid her feelings almost immediately.

She squeezed Connie's hand briefly. "It must've been awful to find her that way. I can't even imagine. Has the cause of death been released yet?"

"Not that I'm aware," Connie said softly.

Jason sat at the other side of the table, and I took the seat next to him. As he unwrapped his sandwich, he asked me, "How was your morning?"

I could feel the heat rise in my cheeks. Despite the conversation carrying on around us and the looks Carla was throwing his way, Jason let me know he was thinking about me.

"It was busy, so that was nice. I also got a call from Mrs. Berry—the play is still on."

"I'm glad," Connie said. "Marielle and the other students will be relieved."

"I am too." Ford was eager to put in his two cents. "I'm looking forward to helping Dave create those sets, especially the library."

"Mrs. Berry mentioned there would be some sort of tribute to Sandra Kelly in the play program," I said.

"That's nice." Connie sipped her tea. "She deserves that."

"She does," Carla said. "After a life riddled with conflict, I hope she now has some peace."

I wanted to know what Carla was talking about. After all, despite not being well-liked by some people, Sandra Kelly had appeared to be a woman who had her life together. But this wasn't the time or the place to ask Carla what she meant.

Chapter Ten

After Jason left to take Carla back to wherever he'd found her and to keep a couple of appointments he had scheduled, I sat down with my sketchbook to work on a design for the footstool for *Beauty and the Beast*. I thought my best bet would to be to dress the actor in black from head to toe and have the footstool at the bottom of the costume—sort of the opposite of the candlestick. But how would I design something the kid could easily move around in? I needed something like a mermaid-type skirt but with more structure at the bottom.

Grabbing my laptop for inspiration, I learned that there were plenty of cute costume ideas for dressing a dog as the enchanted footstool, but not so much for people. I finally found just the thing I was looking for—a Victorian double basket cage underskirt. Customized to hit around the actor's knees, the footstool would flow out from the body and down to the floor. Now...who could help me make a bustle?

Before I could call Grandpa Dave and ask, Max popped in.

Hovering over my shoulder, she looked at the bustle on my screen. "Jeez, Louise! We're not going back to those things, are we?"

"You wore a bustle?" I asked.

"No, and I wouldn't want to." She shuddered. "Imagine getting caught in a lightning storm wearing one of those things. You could get your bum fried off."

"I'm going to use it to make a footstool costume for the play."

"Oh...that's fine then," she said. "Just don't let the kid go out during a storm."

"I won't. I promise." I sketched out a bustle and grabbed my measuring tape to see what dimensions I'd need. "By the way, how did you make it sound as if Frank Sinatra was standing in our kitchen?"

She threw her head back and laughed. "That was the berries, wasn't it? I had it play from Carla's phone. The first sound effects I did, I played on my tablet—I've been practicing at night when no one's here—but I wanted that one to come through loud and clear, so I used Carla's phone."

"It certainly was loud and clear."

"And, in my opinion, the lady is a tramp," Max said, laughing again. "I thought it was particularly funny when you asked me if he was really there."

"You threw me!"

"I know. You recovered well from the faux pas though." She sat on the worktable where Jasmine had leapt up to see her better. "Hello, darling."

"Carla is certainly beautiful, isn't she?" I hated hearing the insecurity in my voice, but I couldn't help it. Carla looked like a movie star. I looked...like me.

"She's no more beautiful than you," Max said. "And I believe Jason made his preference clear."

I didn't say so, but I wished I could feel as optimistic about that as Max did. Before I could say anything else, Ella Peterman came into the atelier.

"I saw that woman here during lunch," she said. "What was she doing here? Is she planning on leasing the shop upstairs?"

"She's definitely not leasing it—she told us so at lunch." I was eager to put Ella's mind at ease—not only because should she and Frank leave, Carla would likely pounce on their vacant spot, but that was one reason.

"That's a relief. Frank and I like it here at Shops on Main, and we aren't ready to leave yet."

"We aren't ready for that either," I said. "Never let anyone run you off from Shops on Main. We need you here, and we need Everything Paper."

"I appreciate that." Her shoulders slumped. "You probably think I'm a silly old woman."

"Nonsense. You're neither silly nor old."

"I heard about Connie finding Sandra Kelly dead in her home." She tsked. "I hate that so much. Connie is a delicate person, you know, and that sort of thing would take its toll on the least sensitive among us."

"Did you know Sandra Kelly?" I asked.

"Sandra and her former husband attended our church for a couple of years. After their marriage broke up, neither ever came back to services. They were welcome, of course, but I imagine they were either afraid they'd run into each other there or the place held too many memories of the two of them together."

"What did you think of her—Sandra, I mean?" I gave a half shrug. "The people at the school either liked her or didn't. There didn't seem to be much of a gray area insofar as their feelings about her were concerned."

"Oh, I liked her well enough. Sandra tended to be more withdrawn and reserved than her husband—that's why it was easier to befriend him."

"Did you ever hear why the couple broke up?" I asked.

"Well, I'm not one to gossip, but—" She leaned forward.

"She might call herself an amateur, but she's suiting up like a pro," Max said.

"There were rumors of infidelity," Ella continued.

"Oooh." Max propped her chin on her fist. "That matches up with what you've already heard. Ask her if it was Sandra or her husband."

"Which..." I hesitated. "Which spouse was rumored to have cheated?"

Ella furrowed her brow. "I believe it was Sandra."

"I'm only asking because some of the kids at school were whispering about an alleged affair between Sandra Kelly and a Mr. Talbot," I said.

Nodding, Ella said, "Talbot teaches math at the high school. That's who I heard Sandra stepped out with, but I later heard that the Talbots reconciled." She shrugged. "I guess not. Oh, well, I'd better get back to Frank." She glanced at my laptop screen. "What're you making?"

I explained that I was hoping to make some sort of cage-like bustle to use for one of the *Beauty and the Beast* costumes.

"I'll send Frank back here," she said. "If you need a cage or a fence built, he can do it."

Before I could say I hated for either of them to go to any trouble, she was gone.

Max grinned. "There you go. Frank can do it."

Ella had no more than closed the door to the atelier when Connie came through the door to the reception area and called out, "Amanda, are you in here?"

"Back here!"

She hurried into the atelier. "Reese Cranston, one of the detectives who worked on Mark Tinsley's murder case called me."

I got up, put an arm around her shoulders, and led her to the worktable. "Have a seat. Everything's gonna be okay."

"I'm not so sure about that." She dropped her face into her hands as soon as she was in the chair.

"Why? What did he say?"

"The police think Sandra was murdered, and they want to question me further," she said.

"Oh, Connie, they can't believe you'd hurt Sandra—or anyone else." I gently patted her back.

"They might," Max said. "She did find the body."

"And immediately called and reported it." Rats. I knew better than to engage with Max when someone other than Grandpa Dave was present.

Connie lifted her head. "What?"

"I said, you immediately called the police and reported it when you found Sandra," I said.

"No, I didn't. I called the ambulance," she said.

"Even better." I spread my arms slightly. "That showed a willingness to help her—to keep her alive. I'm sure they only want to ask you what you saw when you went into her house."

"I'm not so sure." She took a steadying breath. "Detective Cranston is on his way to talk with me now. Would you be with me when he does?"

"Of course." That is, if he'd let me.

That's when Frank barreled through the atelier door. "Hey, Ella said—" He stopped. "Um...are you two doing women things? Talking about feelings or something? I can come back."

Connie stood and smiled slightly. "It's all right, Frank. Come on in." She turned to me. "I'll text you when he gets here."

"All right," I said.

Frank stood just inside the atelier looking awkward until Connie left. Actually, he continued looking awkward even then, but I motioned him over to the worktable.

"She all right?" he asked quietly.

"Yeah...still upset about finding Sandra Kelly's body last night," I whispered.

He squeezed his eyes shut momentarily and nodded. "Sorry. Forgot all about that. It's just that sometimes when Ella tells me things, I let them go in one ear and out the other. Should've paid more attention when she was talking about that."

Max giggled. "What a goof—likable, but still a goof."

"Yeah...well. Shall we look at this bustle?" I asked. "That is why she sent you, isn't it?"

"No." He frowned. "She told me you needed some sort of cage made."

I turned my laptop screen around to face him.

His frown deepened. "You want me to make you a butt cage?"

Max hooted with laughter, and I couldn't hide a grin.

"Actually, I want this at the knees." I showed him the sketch I'd made of the footstool costume.

"Oh, I see what it is," he said. "Do you have a pencil and piece of paper I can use?"

I flipped over to the next sheet of the sketch pad and provided him all my colored and graphite pencils. "Be my guest."

Frank quickly and expertly created the design for a bustle that would tie around the waist but would create the large, square cage at the knees. "See what I'm doing here? You'll need a wide belt with black ribbon to secure the contraption to the waist, so the cage hangs down here where it's supposed to be."

"That's fantastic," I said. "Can you make it? I'll pay you."

"I'd be happy to. Give me the dimensions and tell me how soon you need it," he said.

I told him I'd have the dimensions to him as soon as I found out the height of the actor playing the footstool.

"Great." He grinned. "Let me know."

"Impressive," Max said, as Frank strode out of the room. "When he isn't being treated as a ninny, he's talented and capable."

"I don't think she treats him like a ninny all the time," I said.

She arched her brows.

My phone buzzed. Detective Cranston was here.

Chapter Eleven

Reese Cranston had been promoted to detective for his involvement in solving the murder of Mark Tinsley. I didn't know about Connie, but I was glad to see a familiar face rather than the stern visage of an officer we didn't know.

His blue eyes deepening his crow's feet when he smiled, Detective Cranston greeted us warmly. "Ladies, nice to see you again. Sorry it's under similar circumstances to the last time I saw you."

"Told you." Max gave me a smug nod. "I knew Sandra Kelly had been murdered."

"We don't know that for certain." I hadn't meant to say that out loud. Max had a way of making me discombobulated.

Cranston inclined his head. "Is there somewhere we can talk privately?"

Looking from Cranston to me and back again, Connie asked, "Could Amanda be there too? I'm still shaken up from finding Sandy last night."

"That's fine. This is an interview, not an interrogation."

I could see that Cranston was using what I'd describe as famed negotiator Chris Voss's "late-night FM DJ voice." Was he merely trying to reassure Connie? Or did he think she might be guilty of something?

"Let me put a note on my door telling customers I'll be back in—" She spread her hands. "—fifteen minutes?"

He nodded. "That should work."

"I'll do the same," I said. "We can meet in my atelier. Detective Cranston, would you like some coffee or tea?"

"No, thanks."

The three of us went into the atelier and sat at the workroom table. Connie and I sat on one side, and Cranston sat on the other. He removed a notebook and pen from his jacket pocket.

Max sprawled out in the center of the table, and Jazzy jumped up to lie beside her, rolling over first one way and then the other.

"What's up with the cat?" Cranston asked.

"She doesn't want to miss anything." I picked up Jazzy but glared at Max. "She needs to find a more appropriate place from which to eavesdrop."

"Oh, pooh," Max said. "You're no fun." But she moved onto one of the chairs near the table.

After I placed Jazzy on the floor, the princess joined Max on the chair. When I returned to my seat, Cranston was addressing Connie.

"Tell me what led to your being at Sandra Kelly's home last night."

"Amanda called to let me know that Sandy hadn't shown up for play rehearsal, and she didn't know what to do," Connie said. "Amanda has only been involved with the play for the past few days—she didn't know who else was in charge or any of the particulars. Since my daughter Marielle is in the play, she called to ask my advice."

"Amanda called you to see what she should do?" He scribbled as he asked her to clarify.

"Connie is more familiar with Winter Garden High than I am," I said. "And other people there were getting concerned about why Sandra wasn't at the rehearsal."

"Is he raking us over the coals?" Max demanded. "Because I feel like we're being raked."

I managed to both avoid looking at Max and answering her question. I felt proud of myself. But I did also feel a little heat from those coals myself. What was Cranston getting at?

"When Amanda called, I was getting ready to leave here and head toward the school, so I offered to go by Sandy's house and check on her," Connie said. "When I got there, I saw Sandy's car in the driveway. I went to the door and knocked, but she didn't answer. Concerned, I turned the doorknob. It was unlocked."

"And did you go inside then?" Cranston asked.

"Not right away." Connie glanced at me, and I tried to look reassuring. I'm not sure whether I did or not, but she went on. "My intention was to peep inside and call out to Sandy, but when I opened the door, I saw her lying on the living room floor."

"What did you do at that point?" he asked.

"I called her name. She didn't respond, so I ran inside." Connie placed a hand on her chest. "I bent down and checked to see if Sandy had a pulse. I couldn't find one—I hoped so much that it was merely my inexperience and that Sandy would be fine—so I called 911."

"Do you recall the instructions you were given during the 911 call?"

"I don't know. It's pretty much a blur. The operator asked me to stay on the line, and she asked me questions. She wanted to know if Sandy was breathing, and I said I didn't know." Shaking her head,

Connie said, "I don't know what all she said. It's recorded, isn't it?"

"Of course." Again, with the late-night FM DJ voice. "I just wanted to see what you could remember. Did you see anyone who might've been leaving the area? Any cars speeding away?"

"No. But I was focused on Sandy at the time. I only wanted to get her some help. I told all of this to the officers last night, Detective Cranston. That's all I know." She squeezed my hand. "I could tell when I saw Sandy up close that she was dead—I mean, I didn't want to admit it, but I knew. Her eyes were..." She bowed her head, and her shoulders shook as she sobbed.

I hopped up to get Connie a tissue, and Max moved over behind Connie's chair. She couldn't physically comfort the woman, but she was offering her emotional support. I came back to the table with a box of tissues, placed the tissues in front of Connie, and put a comforting arm around her shoulders. My look at Detective Cranston implored him to go and leave Connie in peace. He didn't heed it.

"I'm sorry for making you go over these minute details again, but I really need to know everything. Anything you can offer might help," he said. "Were there signs of a struggle inside the house?"

"N-no." Connie dabbed at her eyes with a tissue. "At least, there weren't in the living room—that's the only room I went into."

"Signs of a struggle?" I asked. "Are you saying Sandra Kelly was murdered?"

"That appears to be the case." He spread his hands. "The medical examiner notified us that the body showed indications of having been poisoned. He's running the tox screens today." He leaned forward. "I'm asking you both to keep this in the strictest of confidences, at least, until we make an arrest. Can you imagine how panicked the Winter Garden community would be if they believed their children were attending school with a murderer in their midst?"

Gasping, Connie asked, "You believe Sandy was murdered by someone at the school?"

"Most murder victims are killed by someone they know," Cranston said. "We can't rule out the fact that Ms. Kelly's killer is affiliated with the school where she taught."

Before Cranston left Shops on Main, he went to Antiquated Editions to see Ford, his brother-in-law.

Connie and I were silent as we listened to his footsteps ascending the stairs. After a moment, she asked, "Do you really think there's a murderer at Winter Garden High School?"

"You bet your bottom dollar there is!" Max exclaimed.

"I'm sure the students are safe," I said.

"Yeah...me too." Connie retrieved another tissue from the box on the table and daintily blew her nose. "Besides, Detective Cranston said the medical examiner only reported there were indications Sandy was poisoned. The test results aren't back yet, so maybe she wasn't."

"Right." I was quick to throw out my own theory of how—besides having been murdered—Sandra Kelly might've died. "Even if the reports reveal poison in her system, Sandra might've accidentally ingested something toxic."

Max pantomimed pulling things out of the air.

"I hadn't even thought of that." Connie stood and took her tissue to the trash can. "Sandy was most likely not murdered." She took a deep breath. "But from now on, whenever Marielle is at that school, I will be too."

Chapter Twelve

Jason called a couple of hours after Detective Cranston left Shops on Main.

"Kristen's parents hired me to take photos of her at homecoming tonight—the game and the dance," he said. "Would you like to join me?"

"Sure," I replied. "Did she win? Is she going to be crowned queen?"

"Yep. They just found out, which is why I'm going to the game."

I chuckled. "Good for Kristen. She's having a stellar year so far."

"She is. And her parents are chronicling every second of it for her. No pressure, kid!" He laughed.

"You know, I hadn't thought about it, but that is a lot of pressure."

"I think she can handle it," he said. "I've got to run, but I'll pick you up around six-thirty this evening if that's all right."

"I'll be ready."

"What's going on?" Max asked, after I'd spoken with Jason. "What's Kristen going to be queen of?"

"She's the homecoming queen. Her parents hired Jason to come take photos of the event, so he's invited me to tag along to the game and the dance."

"Oh, there's a dance?" Her smile struck me as a bit sad. "That sounds fun."

Remembering she'd died while running down the stairs here to meet her date for a dance, I kinda wished I hadn't said anything. But I knew Max well enough to believe that she wouldn't want me walking on eggshells around her and not talking about what was going on in my life to spare her feelings.

"You'll take pictures, won't you?" she asked.

"Of course!"

She shrugged. "I mean, I'll look at Jason's too, but he's being paid to be all about Kristen—you'll see everything."

"I'll tell you what—I'll do a social media live stream while the homecoming court is being introduced during the halftime show." At least, I hoped I would. I hadn't tried it before, but I figured it couldn't be that hard.

"Really?" Clasping her hands together, she laughed. "Won't that be wonderful? It'll be almost like I'm right there with you! What do I need to do?"

"Let's see," I said. "Kick-off is at seven, so halftime would probably by around eight or eight-thirty. All you'll have to do is go onto my social media page at that time."

"Great! This will be fantastic! I'll get to see Kristen and all her ladies in waiting!"

Her excitement was contagious, and I laughed with her. "It will be fun. Most of them will be wearing dresses from Designs on You."

"And you need to wear something to make yourself stand out as well." She headed over to the pret a porter racks.

"I don't want to be too obvious about making a marketing statement," I told her. "Which is what it would be if I dressed according to the 1950s theme. My initial thought was to wear jeans, a sweater, and boots."

She scoffed. "Um—hello? Making a marketing statement is exactly what you need to do. But don't dress in the '50s theme. The audience will be seeing plenty of that. Choose something from another era."

"Okay, sure. Too bad the RenFaire dress was sold." I grinned. "That would've gotten me some attention."

"Work with me here, would you?" She nodded toward a '40s-style suit.

I took the suit from the rack. It was a navy tweed travel suit with light blue ribbon lacing down the left side of the jacket. The jacket was low cut, but I could wear a light blue sweater shell with it. I'd designed the suit hoping it would appeal to area businesswomen, but so far, dresses—in particular, A-line dresses—had been the most popular items in my pret a porter line.

Stepping behind the screen, I put on the suit and looked at myself in the three-way mirror. Was it too fancy for a high-school football game? Probably, but it was beautiful. And it would be warm. And it would certainly showcase my talent.

"That is absolutely the elephant's eyebrows," Max said, as I turned my head to see how the suit looked in the back. "You'll be causing eyes to pop all over the place."

"Well, I certainly hope not."

Max flicked her wrist. "Yeah, well, just don't slip on any of those eyeballs when you're making my live video thing—I want to be looking at something other than pavement and sky."

After putting the dress I'd been wearing into a garment bag to take home, I reminded Max about the time and site of the live feed. "Don't forget."

"Oh, don't you worry. I'll be right here with my nose pressed to the screen," she promised.

I put Jazzy into her carrier, told Max I'd see her tomorrow, and locked the atelier door. I left through the reception door so I could step across the hall and check on Connie before I left.

"You look fantastic," Connie said when I walked into Delightful Home. "I've never seen you in that suit before. It's gorgeous."

"Thank you. Max encouraged me—" Oops. "I mean, I'm trying to maximize encouragement at the homecoming game this evening to get some new customers." I shook my head. "You know what I mean. It has been a long day." My life would be so much easier if Connie knew about Max.

"It sure has," she said.

"Are you and your family going to the game?"

Shaking her head, she said, "No. I'm picking up food on the way home, and we're going to enjoy a relaxing movie night."

"That sounds great." It really did. I wondered if maybe I could talk Jason or Granda Dave into a movie marathon soon.

"I think so." She twirled her long hair around her finger. "I need to decompress—and, to be honest, hide—so badly."

I gave her a quick hug. "Call me if you need me or if there's anything I can do to help."

At home, I fed Jazzy and then sat at my vanity to touch up my makeup. While I fussed with my appearance, I called Grandpa Dave.

"Hi, Pup. This is a nice surprise."

"I'm glad," I said. "Have you had a good day?"

"Yep. Been finishing up a few things I'm planning to take to the Farmers' Market tomorrow. I'm looking forward to seeing how that goes. What about you?" he asked.

"Detective Cranston came to talk with Connie today. She asked if I could be with her for moral support, and he led us to believe Sandra Kelly was murdered."

"That's terrible. Do you need me to come over and bring a pizza or something? I don't want you to be alone."

"I actually have a date with Jason," I said. "We're going to the football game. I've promised Max that during the homecoming ceremony at halftime, I'll stream live to social media so she can watch it."

"I imagine she's beside herself over that." He laughed. "I'd love to be there with her when she sees it."

"Why don't you? You have a key, and she'd adore it if you were there."

"You know, Pup, I believe I'll take you up on that offer."

I hurried outside when Jason drove up because I didn't want to hold him up. "I haven't been to a high school football game in years," I said as I got into the car.

"They're still the same as you remember."

"How's Carla doing?" I was really proud of myself for asking that and for not acting snotty about her. Of course, acting and feeling were two different things entirely.

"I'd hoped her lunch with us at Shops on Main would cheer her up, but she seemed even more agitated when she left."

I debated whether or not to tell Jason that the police think Sandra Kelly might've been murdered. I finally decided to keep mum because the cause of death was merely speculation at this point, and no one knew anything. My conscience pricked at me and told me it was more about my not wanting Jason to feel the need to console Carla again.

Fair enough. But I'm still not telling him.

Chapter Thirteen

Upon arriving at the stadium, I was once again transported back to my high school days. Seeing the parents and grandparents carrying their bleacher seats and cushions toward the bleachers, the teen girls spotting their friends and squealing with delight as if they hadn't seen each other only hours earlier, and the politicians shaking hands and giving out pens and buttons made me realize Jason was right—very little about the experience had changed.

The band members marched along the edge of the field to a beat hammered out by the percussionists to the fifty-yard-line where they stepped through the fence opening and rose into the bleachers to take their reserved seats. I felt a chill of excitement and squeezed Jason's arm. He smiled down at me and winked.

The scent of popcorn wafted on the air as we found seats overlooking the thirty-yard-line.

"Is this all right?" Jason asked.

"It's fine." I spread out the thick blanket I'd brought for us to sit on—and to snuggle under if we got cold. It was October after all.

"This is nice," he said, sitting on the blanket beside me. "I'm not used to actually being comfortable at these things."

"Amanda! Ms. Tucker!"

I stood to look behind us to see who was calling my name. It was Zoe.

Waving to her, I yelled, "Zoe, hi!"

She was sitting with some girls I'd never seen before. I guessed they must not be associated with the play.

"I'll come talk with you in a little while," she said.

"Okay." I sat back down.

Jason grinned. "You've made friends in the short time you've been a part of the Winter Garden High School world."

"I guess I have."

Moments later, a man's voice came over the loudspeaker instructing us to stand for the playing of the national anthem. As the last strains of the song played, the man asked us to remain standing to observe a moment of silence.

"Sandra Kelly, a beloved teacher of English here at Winter Garden High School, was lost to us far too soon yesterday."

Someone near us gave a snort of derision. I gaped at Jason, shocked at what I'd heard, but he was staring straight ahead.

We observed the moment of silence, the man thanked us, and told us to be seated. Then he welcomed us to the game and made a few other announcements. And then the game began.

Winter Garden High was up seven to nothing just before halftime.

Jason kissed my cheek. "I'm off to record Kristen's big moment."

"Have fun." I watched him carefully wind around other people navigating the stairs and head for the football field. He'd barely made it to the bottom of the bleachers when Zoe came to sit beside me.

"What's up?" she asked. "Is that guy your boyfriend?"

"Yeah, we're dating. He's going to take some photos of the homecoming court." I smiled. "He's a photographer and has a studio in the building where my shop is located."

She nodded. "I've seen him around school some." She fidgeted with the zipper on her jacket. "So...are you still doing costumes for the play?"

"I am. Looks like you're stuck with me."

"I'm glad," she said. "It'd suck if we only had grouchy old Mrs. Berry running the entire show."

"I'm sorry about Ms. Kelly." I wondered again why there was such a division in the way people felt about her. I wanted to ask Zoe what she'd thought of the woman, but I didn't want to ask her here where we could be overheard.

"People around school today were saying she was murdered." She moved the zipper up and down. "Was she?"

Lowering my voice, I said, "I don't think anybody knows what caused Ms. Kelly's death yet. And high schoolers are going to put the most morbid spin on her death that they can. I mean, who wants to listen to a boring story?"

"Yeah, I know. But it wasn't just the kids—some of the teachers were whispering about it too." She shrugged. "They'd hush when they thought any of us got close enough to hear, but we still got the gist of what they were saying."

I didn't know what to tell her. I wanted to reassure her, but I didn't want to lie to her. Other than lying about where she lived, Zoe seemed to be a straight-shooter, and I was sure she could detect a load of hooey—as Max called it—in a millisecond. Before I could respond, one of Zoe's friends shouted to her.

"I'll be back in a minute," she said before climbing the steps.

The band lined up in the end zone with the drum major poised to lead them onto the field. I dug my phone from my purse, quickly logged onto my social media page, and started my live feed.

"I'm at Winter Garden High's homecoming where the marching band is about to take the field. Is anyone watching?"

Grandpa Dave immediately commented, "We are, and we're very excited."

Laughing, I said, "I'm excited too."

"What're you excited about?"

Zoe had returned.

"My grandpa and our friend were unable to attend tonight, so I promised I'd stream the halftime show for them," I said. "Want to say hello?"

"Dave's watching?" she asked.

I nodded.

"Sure, I'll give Dave a shout-out. He's super cool."

I turned the camera toward her.

"'Sup, Dave!" She waved. "Can't believe you're not here in person. You're gonna give everybody the idea you're some old dude who goes to bed before nine o'clock." She leaned closer to the screen to read his response and then threw back her head and laughed. "Listen to this—he says, 'I stayed away because I was a football legend back in the day. I was afraid that if I came, they'd ask me to run the ball.'"

I joined in her laughter. "I've heard he was a pretty good player." I started to turn the phone back toward the field.

"Wait," she said, "he's typing something else. 'Normally, I'd jump right in and help the boys out. But, unlike you kids, I put in a full day's work.' Yeeowch! Your grandpa just gave me a third-degree burn!"

I looked into the camera. "Behave, Grandpa."

He responded with, "Never."

Zoe and I shared another chuckle as I panned the camera over to where the band was marching out to the center of the field before fanning into formation.

Since the homecoming had a 1950s theme, the band kicked off their show with Rock Around the Clock.

"I'd better get back to my friends," Zoe said.

I felt an unreasonable urge to ask her to stay. That was stupid—she should be with her friends. But I couldn't help feeling I'd let her down somehow. Why had she come back? Had she wanted to talk with me about Sandra Kelly? The play? Her mom? Something else?

"Will you come back after the halftime show?" I asked.

"Sure, if I get a chance." She stood as the band segued into a saxophone solo of Blue Moon. "Later, Dave."

"Later, kiddo," Grandpa Dave typed.

After the band's performance, they moved to the right side of the field and softly played the homecoming court on while their introductions were made. Kristen, as queen, was the last to be heralded and her accomplishments were too numerous to mention.

For real, the announcer gave Kristen's name, the names of her parents—Dr. Maria and the Honorable Philben Holbrook—and then said, "Kristen's numerous accomplishments include classically-trained pianist, president of the FBLA, and narrating fairy tales for deaf children."

"I had no idea Kristen was so diversely talented," I murmured, after seeing that my phone's battery was draining and shutting off the live feed.

"She's been training for her college education all her life."

I started at the voice beside me but immediately recognized it as Zoe's. Smiling at her, I said, "It sounds like it."

She nodded. "I guess some of us were lucky enough not to be born to a doctor and a judge, huh?"

"Yeah." I chuckled but felt disconcerted at the bitterness behind her words. "What do your parents do?"

"Dad was a machinist—he died in an accident when I was little. I can't remember him very well."

"And your mom?" I asked.

"She drinks." Zoe burst out laughing at my expression, which I could only imagine reflected the horror I felt. "I'm kidding. She works at the grocery store."

"You really had me going there for a second," I said.

Laughing again, she said, "Yeah, I did."

Was it my imagination, or did this laugh sound even more hollow than the first one? Was Zoe's mom an alcoholic? Had that been what Sandra Kelly had alluded to when she told me she believed Zoe had a sad homelife?

"Are you going to the dance?" I asked.

"Sure, I'll check it out for a few minutes. What about you?"

"I'll be there." I nodded toward the field. "Since Jason was hired to get some photos of the homecoming queen, I'm certain that we'll be there for some if not all of the dance."

After Winter Garden secured the victory with a fourth-quarter touchdown and extra point, Jason suggested we get ahead of the crowd and go on to the gym. He wanted to get some shorts of Kristen before the rest of the students piled into the dance.

"Do you think she'll be there already?" I asked.

"Definitely. No way were her parents going to risk her dress, hair, and makeup getting ruined. I'm pretty sure they kept her in the car until just before halftime and made her go back until the game is over."

"That's terrible!" Aware of other people walking near us, I lowered my voice. "She didn't even get to watch the game?"

"I doubt that bothered her. She doesn't strike me as caring all that much about sports."

I didn't reply, but it still bugged me. From the way Jason talked, Kristen couldn't have watched the game if she'd wanted to...and that was apparently par for the course. I'd never met Kristen's parents—she'd always attended fittings alone and paid with a credit card. How could they be so involved and yet uninvolved? I was anxious to see for myself what the Holbrooks were like.

As soon as we stepped into the gym, Kristen came up and threw her arms around me. "Amanda, hi! Thank you for doing that live feed—it was so cool. I saw the video in the car a few minutes ago. Didn't the band do a fantastic job with the halftime show?"

Before I could respond, Dr. Holbrook pulled her daughter away from me. "Dearest, stop hugging everyone before you crush your corsage." She smiled at me but didn't offer her hand. "I'm Dr. Maria Holbrook. And you are?"

"Amanda Tucker. I own Designs on You."

"Right. Well, you did a marvelous job on Kristen's dress," she said. "It's lovely."

"Thank you."

Dr. Holbrook had moved on. I wasn't sure she'd even heard me. "Phil, stop bending Jason's ear so he can take those photos. We need to wrap this up and be off soon."

"I'd like to stay at the dance for a little while," Kristen said. "Connor told me he'd drive me home."

"You know you need to be at your SAT prep class early in the morning and that you have your recital in the afternoon." Turning to Jason, Dr. Holbrook added, "We won't need you for that, Jason. The videographer is handling the piano recital."

I noticed Jason's jaw tighten, but he didn't say anything. I was guessing he hadn't planned to attend the recital—at least, he hadn't mentioned it to me—and resented the fact that Dr. Holbrook acted as if he were constantly on call for them.

"I won't stay long," Kristen was saying, "but I am homecoming queen. If I'm not here for a little while, it'll look bad."

"Fine. You may stay for one hour after Jason takes your photos," Dr. Holbrook said. "If Connor isn't ready to leave at that time, call and your father will come pick you up."

Connor, a sweet-looking young man, joined us then, and Dr. Holbrook adjusted his tie before he posed with Kristen for a few shots.

As I waited for Jason to photograph the couple, I couldn't help overhearing Dr. Holbrook and her husband murmuring to each other. They were discussing Kristen's academic weaknesses. It appeared she was stronger in math and science than she was in English and history.

"Has anyone said who'll be taking over her English class?" Judge Holbrook asked his wife.

"No, but whoever it is has to be better than Sandra Kelly," she said. "I hate to sound callous, but her death saved me the trouble of getting her fired."

Chapter Fourteen

Grandpa Dave called me just as I was walking into work on Saturday morning. "Hey, Pup. Have you seen Max yet?"

"No, but I'm only now going into the building. Were you able to see the live feed all right?"

"Were we ever!" Max materialized by my side. "It was amazing! We were here, but it was like we were right there with you. Wasn't the band the berries? And all those kids looked lovely."

"Did you hear that, Grandpa?" I asked.

"I did. It does my heart good to hear her being so cheerful and animated. Last night, she wept."

"With joy," Max clarified. "All these years my world has been limited to this house. Now I feel I can go anywhere—or, at least, anywhere you can go."

I sat Jazzy's carrier onto the floor and unlocked the door to the atelier.

"I'd better run, ladies, I see a customer approaching."

"That's right—you're at the farmers' market," I said. "Well, good luck!"

"Our silver fox doesn't need luck—he has talent." Max chuckled.

After getting the cat situated with kibble and water and myself situated with a cup of coffee, I unlocked the reception room door and sat on one of the navy wingback chairs near the window to chat with Max. "Tell me what you liked best about the halftime show."

"I loved it all!" In her excitement, she paced so much that Jazzy could barely keep up. "The band was darb—it took me back to my own high school days, except this band had a lot more talent than we did."

"Oh, were you in the band?" I couldn't picture Max in a band uniform.

"No, but I dated a trumpet player for a very short time." She flicked her wrist. "Tasty set of lips but not much else to recommend him."

I chuckled. "I'm sorry to hear that."

"Not as sorry as I was." She finally sat on the chair beside mine, and Jazzy joined her. "I adored seeing all of the girls—and the boys too, but it was especially fun to see the dresses you created out in the real world."

I agreed with her wholeheartedly on that point. "And what did you think of Zoe?"

"She's lovely—spunky as all get out. She rather reminds me of me at that age."

Smiling, I said, "She reminds me a bit of you too." My smile faded as I remembered her comments about her mom.

"What is it?" Max asked.

"Right after I ended the live feed, Zoe told me her father is dead and that her mother works in a grocery store." I backtracked. "Initially, when I asked what her mom does, she said, 'she drinks.' She played it off as a joke, but I'm not so sure."

"Didn't you say Sandra Kelly told you she thought Zoe had an unhappy homelife?" Max asked.

"She did. And that might explain why Zoe gave me the wrong directions to her house when I offered to drive her home." I sighed. "I feel bad for Zoe's mom. I can't imagine how it must feel to be a single mom and a widower. I wonder if she has any nearby family members or some friends nearby that she can rely on to help out and support her."

"No clue, but she shouldn't be making a bad situation harder by not caring for her child." Max placed an index finger on her chin. "If Sandra Kelly thought that's what Zoe's mother was doing—neglecting her or abusing her—she might've contacted child protective services."

There was a tap on the reception door before an auburn-haired woman opened it and poked her head inside. "Hey, there. I'm just making sure you're open."

"I sure am. Please come on in." I placed a restraining hand on Jazzy in case she decided to bolt. "I keep the door closed so Jasmine here doesn't wander out."

"She obviously missed the big sign on the door pointing that out," Max said. "I'm off, darling. See you later."

"The woman came inside and closed the door behind her. "I don't blame you a bit. I wouldn't want this little sweetheart running off either." As the woman came closer, Jazzy hopped off the chair and sashayed into the atelier.

I stood and properly welcomed the woman to Designs on You before asking, "Are you looking for anything in particular?"

"I saw you at the football game last night." She wandered over to the *pret a porter* racks and began looking at the clothes. "I thought your suit was really cute, and my friend told me who you were. She said you're doing the costumes for *Beauty and the Beast.*"

"That's right. Do you have a child in the play?"

"Not me—my kids are out of school now, thank goodness. My friend does, though." She looked at the price tag on one of the suits, and her eyes widened.

Ignoring her reaction to my prices, I asked, "Did your children go to Winter Garden High?"

"Unfortunately, yes." She blew out a breath. "Sorry. For the most part, it's a good school, but you know what they say about one bad apple spoiling the whole bunch."

"That's true." I nodded. "It seems there's always that one person who ruins everything no matter where you go."

"I mean, I hate to speak ill of the dead, but that Sandra Kelly was a piece of work." She looked over her shoulder to ensure she and I were still the only people in the shop. "They say she was having an affair with one of the math teachers and that she'd give her classes an assignment and then go stand out in the hall and chat with that other teacher for the majority of her class time. Can you imagine?"

"I can't." Even though I'd heard the students talking about Ms. Kelly having an affair, I found it nearly impossible to believe that people would know this was going on and not do something about it. "Didn't anyone report them?"

"If they did, it didn't make any difference," she said. "All I know is that my husband told me he saw Ms. Kelly and Mr. Talbot giggling like a couple of teenagers outside her classroom one day during second period."

"Your husband?"

"Oh...yes, he's the bookkeeper at the school. Sorry, I thought I'd mentioned that."

Shaking my head and trying to maintain my smile, I remembered the exchange between the bookkeeper—Mr. Kramer—and Sandra Kelly the first evening Grandpa and I visited the school. The two obviously didn't get along. That could explain my customer's dislike of Sandra.

She looked at the tag on a brown and gold tweed suit. "You couldn't come down on this price any, could you?"

"Since you're affiliated with Winter Garden High, I'll give you a fifteen percent discount in honor of the play." I thought that was a fair offer.

"I'm afraid that's still too pricey." She forced a brief chortle. "We couldn't work out some sort of trade, could we? I'm a hairstylist."

I managed a fake chuckle of my own. "I'm afraid I'm pretty low maintenance. I could hold the outfit for you, though, if that would help."

"Is there somewhere I can try it on?" she asked.

"Sure." I showed her to the Oriental screen that served as my fitting room.

When she emerged in the suit, it looked as if it had been made for her. And the color was perfect for her skin tone.

"That looks beautiful," I said.

"It does, doesn't it?" She bit her lip. "I'd really like to wear it to my sister's house for Thanksgiving. Would you mind holding it for me until the week before?"

"I'd be happy to."

While she was changing back into her clothes, I walked to the desk and got a notepad and pen. The woman returned before I finished the note. I'd written, Hold For. I held it up so she could see I didn't have the rest filled in.

"It's Diana Kramer," she said. "I really do appreciate your doing this for me. We've—Fergus and I— have..." She shrugged one shoulder. "Had a little run of bad luck these past few months. You know, first one thing and then another."

"I completely understand." I finished writing the note and put it over the hanger's hook. "The suit will be waiting for you when you're ready for it."

She took a card from her purse. "Here. In case you change your mind about making a trade."

The card read Indulgences Beauty Studio and listed an Abingdon address.

Not gonna happen. "All-righty!"

As the woman left and I hung the suit in the atelier, I thought about what she'd said about Sandra and Mr. Talbot hanging around outside their classrooms while they were supposed to have been teaching. While I didn't doubt Mr. Kramer had seen them together on that one occasion, would school officials truly turn a blind eye if they were aware of negligent behavior happening on a regular basis? How were the students expected to learn without a teacher? If it were true that Sandra was inattentive to her students in favor of a tryst, then I could see why some of the parents didn't like her.

Chapter Fifteen

I walked over to Delightful Home to speak with Connie; but since she had customers, I wandered over to her essential oil display. A new blend called Affinity was prominently displayed. Opening the tester bottle, I inhaled the fragrance and detected notes of lavender, bergamot, and some others I couldn't identify. It was a lovely, calming scent, so I took a bottle to the register.

"I love this new blend," I said to Connie.

"So do I. It's wonderful, isn't it?" Rather than ringing up the sale, Connie put the bottle to the side and said, "I'll hold this for you until the end of the day. I don't want you to miss any potential clients on my account." To the two women browsing the shop, she said, "Amanda is the proprietress of Designs on You. She makes the most gorgeous retro-inspired clothes ever."

I thanked Connie and told her I'd be back at the end of the day, but I found her behavior confusing. I could have bought the oil and been back at Designs on You within five minutes. But I supposed she had her reasons for—as Max would say—giving me the bum's rush.

Max still hadn't resurfaced, so I sat at the desk in the reception area with my sketchbook and worked on my ottoman design for *Beauty and the Beast*. Provided Frank could properly fit the "butt cage," I should be able to dress the actor all in black with the exception of the ottoman itself. That piece of the equation was the challenge I was tackling today.

I decided my best course of action would be to basically make two large pillows—one for the front and one for the back tied together at the sides—to fit onto the cage contraption. Needing Frank's advice, I called Everything Paper and asked Ella if she could send Frank to Designs on You when he got time.

"Sure," she said. "I'm anxious to see this thing you two are dreaming up."

With brief laugh, I told her, "I am too."

Thinking I should find out a little more about the person who'd be wearing the costume so Frank could get started on the foundation of the ottoman, I got out the list of primary contacts Sandra Kelly had given me. Of course, her name and phone number were at the top of the page. Mrs. Berry wasn't even listed, so I guessed she hadn't intended to be such a crucial part of the production initially. Zoe's name and number caught my eye, and I breathed a sigh of relief. Not only was she the person most likely to know the name of the person playing the role of ottoman, but she was the one I'd feel most comfortable talking with. I got my phone and called the number.

She answered with a hesitant, almost cautious, "Hello."

"Hi, Zoe. It's Amanda Tucker. I hope you don't mind my calling. I got your number from an info sheet Ms. Kelly gave me."

"Amanda, hi." The relief in her voice was evident. "It's good to hear from you. Did you have fun last night?"

"I did. Did you?"

"Oh, yeah. It was awesome."

I heard a sharp female voice call Zoe's name before her end of the conversation went silent. Had we been disconnected, or had Zoe simply muted the line? A glance at my screen told me the call was ongoing.

Forging ahead, I said, "I'm calling to see if you can give me any information about the person playing the ottoman. A friend is helping me design the costume, and it would help to know roughly how tall he or she is."

"No problem. Carter Anthony is the ottoman, and he's pretty short. I'd say—" Again, complete silence.

"If this is a bad time, we can talk about it on Monday." I certainly didn't want to cause trouble for her. "I'll have to take some precise measurements anyway."

"It's all right," she said. "I'm guessing he's about five-four or five-five."

"Who?" the shrill female voice demanded before Zoe's line was muted again.

My anger burned. "Listen, Zoe, I know my number is in your call log now. Save it and call me any time of the day or night if you need to."

"Yep. Thanks. And right back atcha! I'd better run. Talk to you soon." With that, the call ended.

I sat fuming at the screen and praying Zoe would be all right. Something was definitely wrong about her situation, and I felt compelled to help her.

Connie opened the reception door. "Hi. Is this a good time?"

"It is." I put down my phone. "Your glowing recommendation notwithstanding, those ladies who were in Delightful Home did not come check out my shop."

"Be glad." She placed the bottle of Affinity on my desk and took a seat on the navy chair closest to the desk. "They come in about every Saturday, take any free samples I'm handing out that day, and leave without ever having bought a thing."

I groaned. "That's terrible."

"Tell me about it. That's why I didn't want them seeing me give you a bottle of essential oil."

"I'm paying you for that oil," I said firmly.

Connie's voice hardened slightly. "You are not. You've been wonderful to me and to Marielle. Please accept the oil as a token of my appreciation."

"All right. But we're friends. You know I'll always help you in any way I can."

She smiled. "I do know that. And it means the world to me. I feel the same way about you." Waving her hand, she said, "Let's not get all mawkish, though. What are you working on today?"

As I was showing her my sketch, Frank shouted "hello" from the atelier.

"We're in the front room, Frank," I called. To Connie, I said, "Here's the genius who's going to make this costume work."

Frank bobbed his head from side to side, apparently amused at being called a genius. He pulled the vacant chair over to the desk. "Let's see what you've got there. Hmm...what fabric are you thinking for this?"

I'd only roughed out the shape of the ottoman and hadn't considered the fabric yet. "Since it's an ottoman, tapestry fabric would be the best. It's awfully expensive, though. Let's hope I can find a remnant that will serve our purpose."

Shaking his head, Frank said, "We don't want to put all this work into designing this costume only to settle for whatever cheap upholstery fabric we can find. Why don't you let me paint the fabric? I can coordinate it with the set so the ottoman matches the décor."

"I'm impressed." I knew Frank designed many of the beautiful cards and stationery designs sold at Everything Paper, and he was a talented artist. Still, I felt asking him to custom paint material was too big an imposition. "But I can't ask you to do that. I'm sure it would take a lot of time, and you wouldn't make much money by doing it."

"I don't care. I'm not doing it for the money. I'm doing it for the kids." He grinned. "And for me. I haven't had a challenge like this in ages."

"Well, all right," I said.

Connie chuckled. "This production is turning into a Shops on Main family affair."

"Do you think I could come look at the sets on Monday?" Frank asked.

"I think that'd be great. Plus, I can measure Carter Anthony, the boy playing the part, and get some exact measurements for you."

"Good. I'll look forward to jumping in with both feet," he said. "Even though we need to measure the kid from waist to knee to know how long the supports should be, I can still get started for the framework of the ottoman itself if you can give me the dimensions."

"How about forty inches long—that'll give the piece plenty of room to stick out on the sides without mowing down the other actors on the stage—fourteen inches wide, and fifteen inches from knee to floor?" I measured from my own knee to my ankle to make sure that was close. "We can always add fringe or something if we need to lengthen it, but I don't want Carter tripping over it either."

"Works for me." He stood and moved the chair back in front of the window. "I hope you ladies have a wonderful weekend. I'll see you Monday."

As he left, Connie said, "This high school play is going to end up being as well-costumed as a Broadway musical."

"I wouldn't go that far," I said. "By the way, do you know anything about Zoe Flannagan, our stage manager?"

"No. Why?"

"She's a terrific girl, but Sandra Kelly confided to me that Zoe's homelife might not be the best. I'm concerned about her."

"I'd lost touch with Sandy until recently; but if she was anything like the young woman I knew in college, she would have done everything she could to ameliorate Zoe's situation if she thought the girl needed her help."

Chapter Sixteen

Shops on Main typically closed earlier on Saturdays, and I hoped to get to Winter Garden before the farmers' market ended. I hadn't seen Max since this morning, but I knew that being active so much of yesterday had taken a toll on her.

When I arrived at the Down South Café, one or two of the vendors appeared to be packing up; but otherwise, the event was still in full swing. I spotted Grandpa's table, got Jazzy's carrier from the back seat, and hurried over to say hi.

"How's it going?" I asked, approaching the table.

"Quite well." He reached for the carrier, as Jazzy demanded to be let out. "It's all right, little one, you'll be home soon." Although the air was crisp, he placed the carrier in the shade.

"Thanks," I said. "Would you mind babysitting while I look around?"

"Better make it snappy. We're supposed to close up shop in about twenty minutes."

"Twenty minutes?" That didn't give me much time, but I wasn't about to waste it complaining.

I made a beeline—pun intended—for the Landon Farms Honey table. I'd heard it was delicious and wanted to get a jar. I was also able to snag a bag of apples and an embroidered tea towel during my whirlwind shopping spree.

"Looks like you did all right, Pup," Grandpa said when I returned to his table with my arms full.

"I did. I'm going to take these things to the car, and then I'll be back to help you gather up your things." Holding up the bag of apples, I asked, "Won't these taste great baked with cinnamon?"

"With a dab of whipped cream on top?"

"You bet." I grinned. "Now that we've got tomorrow's dessert figured out, we should probably think about the main course." I went ahead and put my purchases in the car.

On my walk back to Grandpa's table, I slowed when I heard two women discussing someone who could only be Sandra Kelly.

"My daughter was in her class and thought the world of her," one said, "but she did say Ms. Kelly was awfully flirty, especially with Mr. Talbot."

"What is wrong with that man?" her companion wondered. "Why in the world would he risk his beautiful wife and daughter for her?"

"Honey, that's the million-dollar question. Maybe now that she's dead, he'll come to his senses."

The pair went into the café, and I hurried to the other side of the parking lot where Grandpa had already started putting the items he hadn't sold into his truck.

"Give me a hand with this tablecloth, would you please?" he asked.

As I picked up the cloth, I said, "You're not returning home with much. You'll need to bring even more stuff next week."

"Afraid not. I was late to the party—this is the last Saturday Amy is doing the farmers' market." He shrugged. "I wish I'd known about it sooner, but I enjoyed today. And I'm on the vendor list to be contacted if and when Amy decides to host another event. Plus, a few people are interested in having some custom work done—enough to likely keep me busy for the next few months."

"I'm glad. I believe you might have another helper for the play sets." I told him about Frank wanting to attend rehearsal on Monday and how he was helping me with the ottoman costume.

"The more the merrier." He took the folded table-cloth from me and placed it atop a box of smaller items before collapsing the table. "I like Ella, but I feel like she can probably be a bit much to deal with. It'll do Frank good to spend a few evenings away from her."

"I think so too." Lowering my voice, I asked, "Were a lot of people talking about Sandra Kelly today?"

"Not to me. Why?"

I relayed the conversation I'd overheard.

"I've heard the kids joking around about Ms. Kelly and Mr. Talbot while working on the sets," he said. "I didn't know the man was married though."

"I didn't either until Ella mentioned it. She indicated that infidelity with Mr. Talbot was the reason Ms. Kelly's marriage broke up. But, in the end, Mr. Talbot decided to save his marriage." I frowned. "I guess I just imagined that if the two of them were flirting as much as everyone said, things had ultimately not worked out with his wife."

"I'd have thought if Mr. Talbot had wanted to rebuild his marriage, he'd have taken a job somewhere else," Grandpa said.

We finalized our plans for lunch the next day, and I took Jazzy and left. I decided to see if I could find a yearbook for Winter Garden High online. If not, I could try to find one on Monday. But the women I'd heard talking had spoken about how foolish Mr. Talbot was to risk his family over Sandra Kelly. And while I wholeheartedly agreed, I wondered what was so special about him that Sandra would destroy her marriage over him and then engage with him again after he'd already rejected her.

Jazzy was thrilled to be out of her carrier at last. I was afraid she might pout at me all evening, but after a can of her favorite food, I was forgiven.

Grandpa bowed out of the afternoon's play rehearsal. He had promised to call the numbers out at the Bingo game at church that evening.

Not many people did show up at the school. Mrs. Berry busied herself with the few actors who'd arrived, and Zoe came to the backstage corner where I'd set up a portable sewing machine, ironing board, and privacy screen.

"Hi," she said. "How sad are we that we actually showed up here on a Saturday?"

"Pretty sad," I admitted. "Is your mom working?"

"Yeah."

"Did I get you in trouble with her earlier?" I asked.

She shook her head. "Nah, she was just being loud. That's why I kept muting her."

"The joke you made about—"

"About her drinking," she interrupted. "That was dumb of me to say."

"I know you were kidding. But if she needs help or you need help, I'm here."

"And I'm here, if you need help." She grinned. "That's why I'm back here—to see if you need any help."

After thirty minutes, Mrs. Berry called off the practice and said she'd see us all on Monday. I offered Zoe a ride home, but she declined, saying she was going to a friend's house. Once again, I wished she'd trust me with whatever was going on in her life.

Jason was bringing a pizza over later, and we were going to watch a movie. After such a stressful week, we'd agreed a night in would be ideal. I didn't know whether or not it would turn into the movie marathon date I'd hoped for—I'd likely need caffeine to keep from conking out during the first one—but I was definitely looking forward to cuddling on the sofa with Jason.

Inspiration struck, and I called to see if he wanted to bring Rascal with him. That way, he could stay longer and give Rascal more attention. Win/win in my book.

"You're the sweetest girl in the world," he said, "but I was just about to call you."

My heart sank. I could deal with being stood up for work, but it had better not be Carla who was causing him to cancel our date.

"Do you know Blake Talbot?" Jason asked. "He teaches math at Winter Garden High."

"I don't know Mr. Talbot, but I have heard of him." That was putting it mildly.

"He's a really nice guy and was good friends with Sandra Kelly. He called me earlier and asked if we could meet for a beer." He paused. "I'd have felt terrible had I turned him down in light of—"

"Oh, no," I interrupted. "You should absolutely go be with your friend."

"You really are the best. I'll call you later."

After ending the call, I wondered why Jason hadn't mentioned his friendship with Blake Talbot before now. Night before last, he'd only been concerned with telling Carla about Sandra Kelly's death—he'd said nothing about reaching out to Blake Talbot. Had he reached out to Mr. Talbot? What else might Jason be keeping to himself?

Now that I knew Jason wasn't coming over, I changed into my pjs, made myself some pasta, poured a glass of sweet tea, and sat at the kitchen table with my laptop. An online yearbook search quickly provided a photo of Blake Talbot, who also coached the school's golf team. The man was a far cry from the Greek god model I'd been anticipating. I mean, he wasn't ugly, but the balding blond man with the crooked nose and lopsided smile didn't inspire me to fantasize about running toward him on a deserted beach with my arms outstretched. Maybe he had a magnetic personality. I'd have to come up with a way to find that out for myself.

That task completed, I set out to see what else I could learn about Max's sister's lineage. I started with Dot's daughter, Maxine. Unfortunately, I didn't get far. Little Max died from measles when she was only eight years old.

Dwight, Dot's son, was two years Maxine's junior. I discovered that he began working in an auto mechanic shop at age sixteen, married Penny Sue Delp at age nineteen, and had a daughter in 1959. Dwight would've been twenty at the time. I teared up a bit when I saw that the name of his first child was Maxine. He and Penny had two more children—a son named after his father in 1961 and a daughter named Grace in 1963.

Armed with this update for Max, I turned off the laptop. Refilling my tea glass, I decided that I didn't have to forego movie night because Jason wasn't here. I went into the living room, curled up on the sofa, and was soon joined by Jazzy—who, by the way, was a wonderful movie companion even if she did sleep through the entire thing. In fact, her soft, rhythmic snoring was so hypnotic that I dozed off too.

When I woke up at a little past midnight, I saw that I'd missed a call from Jason at around ten-thirty. Since he hadn't followed up with a text and it was too late at night to return his call, I decided to reach out to him in the morning. Blake Talbot must've had plenty to say. I hoped Jason would tell me what it was. If nothing else, maybe he could explain his friend's relationship with Sandra Kelly.

Chapter Seventeen

The next morning after Jazzy and I had our breakfast, I called Jason.

"Good morning, beautiful," he answered.

"I'm sorry I missed your call last night," I said. "I fell asleep early."

"I should've expected as much—you've had an exhausting week. Would you let me make up that movie and pizza date to you this evening?"

"Sure." Fingers crossed I could stay awake this time. "Is Mr. Talbot all right?"

"He's getting there, but it's not easy. He and Sandra had a...a complicated relationship."

"So I've heard," I said wryly.

"Actually, it isn't what you've heard." His tone had taken on a slight edge.

"I'm sorry. I didn't mean to be insensitive."

He sighed. "You're not saying anything that everyone else in Winter Garden isn't at least thinking."

"And, yet, I imagine you didn't expect me to rush to judgment too." I apologized again.

"That's okay. We'll talk about it this evening."

I was still feeling pretty rotten when Jazzy and I got to Grandpa's house.

"What's the matter, Pup? You look like three rainy days."

As I let Jazzy out of her carrier and hung up my jacket, I explained about my canceled date with Jason because he needed to meet up with Blake Talbot and how I'd put my foot in my mouth about Talbot's relationship with Sandra Kelly.

"I feel like a jerk for jumping to conclusions."

Sitting at the table coring the apples I'd bought at the farmers' market, Grandpa shook his head. "Don't be too hard on yourself. Everybody at that high school—adults and kids alike—think those two were carrying on. He might be feeding Jason a line in order to try to salvage what's left of his reputation."

I washed my hands before grabbing another corer and sitting down to help with the apples. "I hadn't thought of that. But it makes sense. With Sandra dead, he could be trying to distance himself from her, not only for the sake of his reputation but for that of his marriage." I pressed the corer into an apple and the juice oozed out onto my fingers. "According to Ella, Mr. Talbot is the reason Sandra Kelly's marriage broke up. In the end, Talbot chose to stay with his wife. That's what doesn't make sense to me—why would either of them entertain any sort of relationship whatsoever given their history?"

He shrugged. "Could be they were moths to flames. Even if what Talbot told Jason is true—that they weren't having an affair—they were sure spending enough time together to give folks that impression...even at the expense of some of their students' education, if the tales are to be believed."

"Exactly." I lifted the core from the center of the apple. "If they weren't having an affair, why would Talbot risk his marriage—a marriage he'd already chosen over Sandra once?"

"I suggest you hear Jason out, but don't be naïve. And don't beat yourself up." He wagged the apple corer he held. "You've never been judgmental, but you've always been discerning. Remember that."

Drawing my brows together, I asked, "Don't those two words mean the same thing?"

"Nope. Judgmental people are mean. Discerning people see through the crap and make wise choices." He nodded at the cored apples. "Let's make the filling for these beauties and get them in the oven."

While waiting for Jason and Rascal to arrive, I sat at my vanity and touched up my makeup. I'd already fed Jazzy and had put her food bowl in the cabinet under the sink. I knew from the past experience of my college roommate that cat food can make dogs very sick, and I wanted Rascal to enjoy his visit.

Jazzy lay on my bed glaring at me.

"What?" I asked. "You seemed to have fun with Rascal the other night. I think you'd like him if you'd give him a chance. He's really sweet."

She gave me a slow blink before turning her head.

"All right, sure, he's a little goofy...but he means well."

The stubborn feline refused to acknowledge I'd said anything.

Blowing out a breath, I reminded her, "You gave Max a chance, and you love her." And then I realized this is what my life had become—spending most of my days talking with a ghost and trying to reason with a cat. Somewhere there was a padded room with my name on it.

I was saved from further self-analysis when Jason rang the doorbell. After kissing him hello, I led him into the kitchen. Rascal happily tagged along.

"If you don't mind grabbing the plates, I have a treat for Rascal," I said.

"You didn't have to do that." His smile told me he was pleased I had.

I retrieved the chew toy and bag of bacon flavored treats I'd bought at the grocery store earlier in the week. Holding the bag up I asked, "Are these all right for him to have?"

"Yep. They're some of his favorites."

Rascal looked from one of us to the other, almost as if we were playing a tennis match.

I opened the bag and gave Rascal a treat. "I'll give you another one later. Jason and I are hungry too."

"Mind if we eat here at the table and put the movie on hold?" Jason asked, as he put the plates and forks on the table. "I'd like to talk with you before we get engrossed in the film."

"Sure. That'll be great." I opened the refrigerator door. "What would you like to drink?"

"Water with lemon is good for me."

I poured us each a glass of water and put a spritz of lemon juice in each one. "What would you like to talk about?" I asked, placing the glasses on the table and then grabbing the pitcher before sitting down.

"Blake Talbot." Jason looked around to see that Rascal had taken his chew toy to the rug in front of the sink. Apparently satisfied that the dog wouldn't drive us crazy while we ate, he opened the pizza box. "I hope you like chicken alfredo on a hand-tossed crust."

"I love it." I took a slice and put it onto my plate. Anxious as I was to hear what Jason had to say about Blake Talbot, I knew I needed to listen closely and choose my words even more carefully.

Once Jason had served himself a slice of the pizza, he took a long drink of water, topped off his glass from the pitcher, and then leaned closer. "I'm sorry if I sounded harsh over the phone this morning. You're the sweetest woman in the world, and I know you'll give Blake the benefit of doubt once I've explained his situation to you."

"Of course." I stuck a forkful of pizza in my mouth. It was far better to eat than to talk, especially when I had a million questions—the main one of which was why in the world would Talbot sneak around with a woman who'd already nearly cost him his marriage once before?

"When I got to the bar, Blake had already put a couple of beers under his belt. I ordered a light brew, and we moved to a corner table where we could talk. He said he felt responsible for Sandra Kelly's death." He let that bombshell lie there on the table between us while he dug into his food.

"Why would he feel that way?" I asked.

Did Talbot believe Sandra's ex-husband had killed her because he thought the two of them were back together? Was Sandra's ex being questioned? After all, the police typically look at people closest to a murder victim. Like an ex. Or a current lover.

"Talbot told me he believed the school's bookkeeper was embezzling from various programs," Jason said. "He's Winter Garden High's golf coach, and he noticed there were some discrepancies in the golf account."

"Did he report the discrepancies to the principal?"

He shook his head. "He said it was only around twenty dollars, not enough to be concerned about at first."

"I imagine he went back and found other inconsistencies?" I asked.

"He did, and he began noticing them going forward as well."

"Not to sound like a broken record, but why didn't he report it?" I sipped my water.

Jason tossed a bit of pizza crust to Rascal, who gobbled it up. He was afraid that without further evidence against the bookkeeper, he'd be accused of stealing the money himself and reporting it in an effort to cover his tracks. So, he turned to Sandra for help."

"Why in the world would the man ask the woman it was reputed he'd had an affair with to help him? Didn't he realize that would be akin to throwing kerosene on an open flame?" I realized around that point that I should've stuffed another bite of pizza in my face, but I'd already blurted out the questions.

"That's basically what I asked him," he said.

"Really?" That's good.

"Yes. I'd heard the rumors too. Blake even admitted they'd had an affair and that the only reason he didn't divorce his wife for Sandra was to avoid breaking his daugter's heart."

"Wow. I'm surprised his wife didn't insist on his taking a job at another school." I cut into my pizza with the side of my fork. "Plus, it must've been hard for both him and Sandra to set aside their feelings and work together."

"He'd been looking for another job when he began to suspect the bookkeeper of embezzling. As to why he didn't ask for help from someone else, Blake said that after his affair with Sandra last year, the rest of the staff treated them both like pariahs."

"And he was afraid no one else would help him," I said. "That's sad."

"Not only that, he was scared they'd be the very ones to turn the finger back toward him, implicate him in the embezzlement, and get him fired."

"But how was Sandra going to help? Wouldn't the other faculty members think the two of them were in on the embezzling scheme together?" Jazzy startled me by rubbing around my ankles. I looked down and saw that she was sitting at my feet watching Rascal from a safe distance.

"Blake thought that if they both could find evidence of embezzling, then they could go to another person—he was considering the band director because even though the man wasn't friendly to either of them anymore, Mr. Moody wasn't nasty to them. Plus, they felt him to be an honest man who'd take them seriously enough to at least give his accounts a closer look."

I frowned. "But that still doesn't explain why Blake feels responsible for Sandra's death. The police haven't even officially ruled it a homicide yet, have they?"

"I don't know." He shrugged. "But they've questioned Blake, and he's miserable because he believes that if he hadn't gone off playing Sherlock Holmes, Sandra would still be alive."

"He believes the bookkeeper killed her?" I asked.

"He doesn't know. By the time he'd told me that much, he was pretty drunk," he said. "I'd switched to club soda after the one beer, so I drove him home."

Wincing, I said, "Can't imagine his wife was delighted when he came in sloppy drunk."

"I'm guessing not. He went in alone. I only waited to make sure he got inside okay before I left."

I squeezed his hand. "You're a good friend."

"I try. Please tell me the movie you've chosen is funny."

"Oh, yeah. It's a real knee-slapper called Terms of Endearment." At his look of horror, I laughed and told him I was only kidding.

Chapter Eighteen

Max met me at the door on Monday morning. "What's up, Buttercup?"

"I'm so relieved to see you," I said. "I wish I could give you a hug."

"I'm happy to see you too," Frank said, stepping out of Everything Paper just as I'd made my proclamation to Max. "Why are you relieved, though? That seems an odd choice of words."

"I'm...um...relieved you're willing to help out with the play." I gave Frank an awkward smile as Max chortled. "I'm afraid I'm in over my head with this entire costuming situation."

"Now, don't you worry." He patted my shoulder. "You're more capable than you know, and you have lots of help. We're gonna put on the best play Winter Garden has ever seen."

"Thank you. I truly appreciate the vote of confidence." I went on down the hall, unlocked the door, and placed my tote and Jazzy's carrier on the floor. After I'd closed the door, I let Jazzy out of the carrier and stored my tote in the bottom drawer of the filing cabinet.

"Frank is sweet, isn't he?" Max said, as I continued getting ready to start my workday. "He never said or did much—at, least not here—before you moved in. You and Dave have been good for him."

"Grandpa more than me." I put some kibble in Jazzy's bowl.

"True. He didn't have much male companionship here. Ford, as you've seen, stays upstairs to himself except for trips to the kitchen for coffee and snacks."

"Even he has taken an interest in the play," I said, "although I don't believe he would have if Grandpa hadn't roped him into it."

She grinned. "You two have breathed new life into this place...and no one appreciates it more than I do."

"You've been a real blessing to us too. I've been wondering, would you like your own social media page?"

Her eyes widened. "What? How? Are you kidding me?"

"Not at all. We could set you up a free e-mail account and use it to create your social media profile. You could use the in-platform messaging system to video chat with Grandpa and me anytime you'd like."

"A video chat—" She squinted. "Like with the football game?"

"Similar, but it would be private, and we could carry on a conversation. Here, I'll show you...that is, if he's online." I logged onto my social media account on my phone, saw that Grandpa was indeed online, and sent a video chat request.

When he accepted the request, his face filled my screen.

Max gasped. "Dave!"

"Good morning, ladies." He raised his coffee mug in salute. "You two are obviously more awake than I am—and you both look radiant, I might add."

"Thank y—"

"You can see us?" Max interrupted. "Both of us?"

"I can. Now, I imagine if someone else was here, that person could only see Amanda." He shrugged. "Unless they were a member of the family or other-wise...um...gifted."

"How absolutely marvelous!" Max clasped her hands together. "Amanda is going to get me onto social media. Once again, she's broadening my hori-zons. Isn't she wonderful?"

"I'm partial to her." He winked at me. "Did Jason talk with you about Talbot last night?"

"He did." I took a seat at the worktable and propped the phone against a pattern book.

"What about Talbot?" Max asked. "What have I missed?"

I quickly explained that Jason had told me Talbot and Sandra had not resumed their affair but were working together to gather evidence against the bookkeeper. "They believed Kramer was embezzling from the school."

"I'm sorry, Pup, but that story sounds a tad fishy to me."

"I'm with Dave," Max said. "I wonder if maybe the guy was running his phonus balonus by Jason to see if anyone would buy what he's selling."

"Yeah," Grandpa said, "I'm afraid Talbot might simply be trying to shift blame for Sandra's death onto someone else."

After talking with Grandpa, I set up Max's email account and then created her social media page using a cartoon flapper as her profile pic. She wasn't terribly interested in the email account, but she was all about filling out her profile information. As she input her likes and joined online groups, I did two things: I worked on my remaining costume sketches for *Beauty and the Beast*, and I wondered if I'd come to regret creating this monster that was Max Online.

"I've just joined a group of people who enjoy silent movies," she called. "And a group of people who love musicals." She paused. "I suppose now I need to watch some musicals."

"Okay," I said absently."

"Joined a book group! And another one..."

"Wonderful."

Connie opened the door to the atelier and quickly stepped inside. Seeing Jazzy lying on the table near Max's tablet, she gave the cat a pat on the head. "What's wonderful?"

"The fact that I'm creating the design for the last really difficult costume for the play." I thought I handled that pretty smoothly. "Have you been busy this morning?"

"Not terribly," she said. "You know the old saying about rainy days and Mondays—and today, we have both. But I imagine traffic will pick up after lunch."

"Did you have a nice weekend?" I asked, sketching a handle onto the chipped teacup costume.

Connie nodded. "It was peaceful. We ordered in both Saturday and yesterday and binge watched all the Toy Story movies."

Max had moved closer to us. "What's that? Is it something you think I'd like?"

At least, she'd stopped manipulating the tablet while Connie was in the room. The poor woman had suffered enough stress over the past week without thinking that either my tablet had a mind of its own or that she was going crazy.

"I love those movies," I said.

"So do I." She gave me a slight smile. "Even though I do always cry at some point while watching them."

I laughed. "Me too."

"Just wait until you're a parent," she said. "Then those outgrown toys take on even more significance."

"Outgrown toys?" Max mused. "Sounds weird, but if you'll find it for me, I'll watch it."

I gave her the briefest of nods before asking Connie, "Had you heard the rumors about Sandra Kelly and Blake Talbot?"

Her smile faded. "I had."

"Did you believe them?"

Taking a moment and seemingly choosing her words carefully, she said, "The rumors were compelling—coming from so many different sources—but I try to give everyone the same consideration I'd want them to give me."

"Judge not...?" I asked.

"Right. It's easy to look at something standing outside of it and believe we know everything necessary to make a determination about it," she said. "But, in fact, we know little about another person's life—only what they choose to show us."

"That's true." I glanced at Max to see that she also was at least considering the wisdom of Connie's words. "I heard that Mr. Talbot denies having an affair with Sandra—currently, anyway—and that he and Sandra were trying to right a wrong."

"What wrong?" Connie asked.

"They thought someone at Winter Garden was stealing."

"That makes sense." She slowly nodded. "When we were in college Sandy was the victim of identity theft. She had the worst ordeal trying to get everything sorted out and her credit repaired. She'd have done everything in her power to take down a thief. Do you think—?"

Holding my gold coloring pencil between my middle and index fingers, I raised my hand slightly. "Let's not jump to conclusions. Remember, Detective

Cranston only said it appeared Sandra was murdered. "That hasn't been confirmed."

"Yes, it has," she said. "He called me this morning and said the poison had been identified. It was nicotine."

"Is there any way Sandra could've accidentally poisoned herself?" My mind scrambled to figure out how someone could inadvertently smoke too many cigarettes, but I drew a blank.

"No way. Her grandmother died of lung cancer after chain smoking for years. It made Sandy physically ill to even be in the same room with someone who was smoking."

"I'm sorry. You came over to have a nice chat, and I've gone and made it stressful for you," I said.

"No, you didn't. I won't breathe easily again until Sandy's killer has been arrested." She stood. "Hopefully, Blake Talbot can help the police make that happen. I'll talk with you later."

"How do you kill someone by smoking at them?" Max demanded after Connie left. "Is that even a thing?"

"I suppose the killer could do her in with secondhand smoke, but that wouldn't be a speedy or effective cause of death."

Placing her hand on her chest like a Shakespeare-an-trained actor, she said, "I shall see if there's a murder club on here who can tell us how one would smoke another person to death."

"Please don't." I pinched the bridge of my nose and closed my eyes. Yeah, online Max might turn out to be a total nightmare.

"You're right. Had I been clever enough to find a way to smoke someone to death, I might join a murder club to see if anyone brought it up. My asking about it could sound the alert." She began to pace. "Where can we discover methods of smoking people to death?"

I lowered my hand and opened my eyes. "There are other forms of nicotine, you know. The killer wouldn't necessarily have to use cigarettes."

She looked at me as if I were crazy. "Nicotine in something other than a gasper? You mean, a pipe?"

"No, I'm talking about nicotine patches, for example. They're designed to help people quit smoking."

"A patch filled with nicotine to get you off gaspers?" She threw back her head and laughed. "What do they give people who want to get off the hooch—a martini?"

Rather than follow Max down that rabbit hole, I gave her a shrug and turned my attention back to the teacup. "What border do you think I should put on the cup?"

"The same one you put on the pot. They're a set." Anchoring her hands to her hips, she asked, "Are you going to help me figure out how this nicotine poison thing works, or not?"

I put down my pencil and opened my laptop.

Chapter Nineteen

Frank rode with Grandpa and me to the school after work, so I didn't get to tell Grandpa about nicotine poisoning being the cause of Sandra Kelly's death or about the case studies Max and I discovered online. The yuckiest instance of poisoning we read about was where someone had soaked cigarette butts in water and then poured the water into something the victim drank. I believe the beverage used was some kind of hard liquor, but I found it hard to believe that anything could cover the taste of something as nasty as cigarette butt water.

Grandpa glanced over at me as he stopped at an intersection and said, "I accepted a social media connection from your friend Max today."

Before I could respond, Frank said, "Ella is into all that stuff, but I don't have much use for it myself. Oh, I do reckon it helps with the business—we see more people come in when we offer specials or discounts online—but I don't feel the need to let people

"

know what I'm doing every minute or to show them what I'm having for lunch." He grunted. "Today, they'd have gotten to see a picture of a pack of peanut butter crackers."

He went on to soliloquize the pros and cons of social media the entire way to Winter Garden. I was bored silly but impressed, nonetheless. I'd never heard Frank talk so much about anything.

When we arrived at the school, Frank was the first person out of Grandpa's truck. I'd left Jazzy at Designs on You with Max and would get her when Grandpa dropped me back off. Ella had taken her and Frank's van home, so Grandpa had said he'd give Frank a lift after we finished up with rehearsal.

I hung back with Grandpa as Frank barreled through the door. "I believe he's excited about this."

"You think?" Grandpa grinned a he opened the door for us.

I spotted Zoe first thing. She was standing in the hallway talking with a haggard-looking woman with dishwater blonde hair. Zoe tried to walk away from her, but the woman gripped her arm.

Hurrying toward them, I said, "Hi, Zoe. Is everything okay?"

The woman released Zoe's arm and turned baleful brown eyes on me. "Who're you?"

"I'm Amanda Tucker. I'm doing costuming for the play." I offered my hand but lowered it again when the woman ignored it.

"I'm Maggie Flannagan, and I'm trying to have a private conversation with my daughter."

I looked from Maggie Flannagan to Zoe.

"I'll be there in just a minute, Ms. Tucker," Zoe said.

"All right." I turned and headed toward the auditorium, but I walked slowly and kept my ears attuned to the hissed conversation behind me. If Zoe so much as gasped, I was going back.

"Everything good with Zoe?" Grandpa asked softly, falling into step beside me.

"I don't know. She and her mom are having a pretty tense conversation." I inclined my head. "Of course, Mom and I also have heated discussions. But after Sandra mentioned she didn't think Zoe had a happy life at home, I guess I'm more inclined to look for signs of abuse or neglect."

"Zoe's a smart girl, Pup. If she needs help getting out of a bad situation, she'll let you know."

"Maybe," I said. "But I want to make sure she has plenty of opportunities."

Zoe joined us in the auditorium a few minutes later.

"Hey, I'd like to talk with you after rehearsal," I told her.

Her face hardened. "About what?"

"About the possibility of your helping out at Designs on You on Saturdays. I could use some help, but I don't want to suffer through job applications and interviews, especially since the job is for only one day a week—and not even a full day at that." I watched her expression relax and become hopeful. "Would you be interested?"

"Definitely!" She smiled.

"Good," I said. "We can talk more about that later. At the moment, I need for you to round up our ottoman actor."

"On it!"

As Zoe hurried off to find Carter Anthony, I pulled Frank away from Grandpa and Ford long enough to get an idea of how he wanted to create the cage part of the costume.

Zoe returned with a boy half a head shorter than she was. As I measured Carter from hip to ankle and from shoulder to hip, Frank walked around the two of us muttering to himself.

Once I'd finished noting the measurements, I asked Frank his opinion.

"Now that I've met the young man who'll be tackling the role of this footstool and have seen the living room set, I'm poised to help make an exquisite costume." He extended a hand for Carter Anthony to shake.

The young man with the sweet elfin face and square glasses looked at Zoe and me as he shook Frank's hand with more than a little hesitancy because, in the blink of an eye, Frank Peterman had morphed into Pierre-Auguste Renoir. Or Edith Head. Or some strange combination of the two.

"Thank you, Frank," I said.

"Happy to help. I'll work on my design this evening when I get home." He jerked his thumb over his shoulder. "Now, I need to go see if Dave and Ford need me. See you later."

Zoe scrunched up her face after Frank left to join the other men in the hallway where they were working on the sets. "He's kinda weird."

I smiled. "I believe he's delighted to be doing something challenging."

"Cool."

"Do you need me for anything else, Ms. Tucker?" Carter asked.

"No, thanks. I appreciate your patience, and I think you're going to love your costume."

He nodded. "Cool."

I was glad to see the younger generation—even though they weren't that much younger than I—still used our most common byword.

"So, who's the next costume on our list?" Zoe asked, as Carter rejoined the rest of the cast.

"It's the teacup," I said. "Is Joey Conrad here?"

"Yeah, I saw him and his mom in the hall earlier."

As Zoe went to track down our modern-day Dennis the Menace, I recalled my previous experience when he visited Designs on You. He'd brought his two ferrets—Biscuit and Gravy—into the shop in his backpack. They'd escaped and ran all over the first floor of Shops on Main, leaving quite a bit of excitement in their wake before Joey and his mother caught them.

Joey came in wearing his denim backpack along with jeans, a red and white striped shirt, and red sneakers. He beamed up at me. "I know you. You're the lady who makes dresses."

"That's right, and I'm going to make your teacup costume." I nodded toward the backpack. "I hope Biscuit and Gravy are at home watching TV today."

"Heck, no. They're right here. Wanna see?"

"No—" I began, but it was too late. Joey was handing me Biscuit, the albino ferret.

The cute little creature was too curious to be held, and it scurried over my shoulder and down my back. I squealed as Joey broke into a fit of giggles and Zoe dove for—but missed—the ferret.

By this time, Joey was holding the brown ferret—Gravy—who immediately spotted his companion dancing sideways across the back of the stage. Not wanting to miss out on the fun, Gravy scrambled out of Joey's arms, grabbed my yellow tape measure, and skittered off to show Biscuit what it had stolen.

"Hey! Bring that back here!" My protest fell on deaf ears.

Alerted by the commotion, Sarah Conrad hurried over to try to ameliorate the situation. "Joey, I told you to leave Biscuit and Gravy at home."

"Aw, Mom, they're my best friends. They don't like to be left out of stuff."

With a sigh, she told him, "Help me round them up."

"Zoe, please close the door going into the hallway but ask the men first if either of the ferrets came out there," I said."

"On it," she said, making a beeline for the hall.

Hearing a scream, Sarah and I shared a quick look and then decided that was where we were most likely to find the ferrets. And we did—one of them anyway.

Gravy had lodged itself inside Kristen's v-neck t-shirt and was struggling to get out.

"Get this thing off me!" Kristen shrieked. "It's in my bra!"

"Do you blame it?" one of the guys joked.

"Hey, it has great taste, Kristen," another teased.

"That's enough," I said. "Kristen, calm down and walk over here with me."

"It's scratching me!"

"Calm down." I put my hand on her back. "Your panicking is scaring it."

"I'm scaring it?" she demanded. "Whose side are you on?"

"Yours, Kristen." I rolled my eyes at Sarah Conrad who suppressed a smile as she shielded Kristen from onlookers. I took hold of Gravy. "Kristen, can you unhook your bra for a second?" Although I'd whispered the words, a whoop went up from the boys. "Guys, that's enough!"

Kristen shook her head. "No way am I undoing my bra here."

"Then we're either going to have to walk over there to the fitting area or go to the ladies' room," I said.

"No!" She was adamant.

"Sweetie, you need to help us," Sarah said softly. "Gravy is stuck."

"I don't want to touch it." But she did manage—through her shirt—to get Gravy's tiny paws extricated from her bra.

I lifted Gravy out and handed him to Sarah. "One down."

"Seems like déjà vu, huh?" she asked.

With a smile, I resumed looking for Biscuit. I also kept an eye out for my measuring tape that Gravy had absconded with. Dare I ask Kristen if it's inside her shirt? One look at her murderous expression told me no...she'd return it later if she found it.

When we went back to the fitting area, Joey was sitting on a stool holding Biscuit. My tape measure was there on the floor. I was guessing Biscuit had taken the tape away from Gravy and hightailed it in the other direction.

Sarah held her hand out for the backpack. Joey gave it to her and hugged Biscuit before turning the ferret over to his mother.

"You can't keep taking these ferrets everywhere you go," Sarah told her son. "One day, something bad is going to happen to one of them."

He nodded. "I know. I heard that girl screaming about Gravy getting in her bra. I never meant for him to get caught in a booby trap."

Zoe burst out laughing and gave Joey a high five.

"You know, I bring my cat to work with me every day," I said. "I bring her in a carrier. I bet you could find a small carrier for Biscuit and Gravy, Joey. They could see what's going on and be right there with you, but they wouldn't be able to run away and maybe get hurt."

"Or wind up in booby traps," Zoe added.

"He could leave them home like I tell him to," Sarah said.

We all knew Joey wasn't going to do that.

Chapter Twenty

I insisted Grandpa take Frank home before taking me back to Shops on Main to get my car. He knew me well enough not to argue, even though he was going a fair distance out of his way to take Frank home first.

"Ella probably has his dinner waiting," I said.

"Maybe." Frank smiled slightly. "Probably. She's a good woman, you know. I probably don't show her enough appreciation."

I thought it was more likely the other way around, but I didn't say so. We dropped Frank off, waved goodbye, and headed back to Shops on Main.

"So, what's on your mind, Pup?"

Since we hadn't eaten before rehearsal, my stomach was beginning to think my throat had been cut. "Let me buy us some food to take back to the shop. I want to talk with you...and with Max, if she's there."

When we walked into Designs on You with burgers and fries, I told Grandpa, "This place always seems kinda eerie when no one else is here."

"Yeah. You'd almost think it was haunted." He smirked.

Max appeared in front of us and jutted out her hip. "Did I hear someone talking about me?"

"Almost, darlin'," he said. "Almost."

"Was it true?" She pursed her lips. "If not, make it an outlandish tale. I want to be remembered."

"I don't know how anyone who'd ever met you could forget you, Max," Grandpa said.

"Neither do I." I placed the bag of food on the worktable. "I need to talk with you both."

"Uh-oh." Max raised her brows. "This sounds serious."

"It is. A little." I put my straw in my drink and took a sip of my soda before announcing, "I've hired Zoe to work here on Saturdays." I watched them both to gauge their reactions, but I was most interested in what Max thought.

"All right." Grandpa drew out the words, as if he was wondering why I'd deemed that a serious topic of conversation.

"After seeing her in the hall with her mom and getting the impression that their relationship is particularly tense, I thought about what you said, Grandpa. If Zoe's situation is bad, maybe she'll confide in me. But only if she trusts me." I unwrapped my burger. "She isn't going to trust me if she doesn't know me."

"So, you hired her to work with you one day a week," Max said. "That makes sense."

"That, and I can definitely benefit from the help. I'll have to go pick Zoe up before work on Saturday mornings," I said, "and take her home at the end of the day, since she doesn't have transportation. I mean, I suppose she could ask her mom to bring her, but I don't really see her doing that."

"Can you afford it?" Grandpa asked.

"I can since it's for only for four hours a week. I told her that when I become better established—and she gets her own car, although I didn't point that out—maybe we can negotiate something steadier." I turned my attention to Max. "I hate to tie up our Saturdays like this--"

"But if it might help the girl, then you should definitely do it," Max interrupted.

I smiled at her. "Thanks. I knew you'd understand. Plus, she'll have to get her mother's permission, and based on the way the woman behaved at the school, she might not allow Zoe to work here."

"Hey, maybe Zoe could be my friend on social media." Max smiled at the thought. "I have ten people liking me already, including the two of you."

"Just wait," Grandpa said. "Before you know it, you'll have thousands of people liking you. I mean, who wouldn't like you?"

"Truer words were never spoken, Dave." She grinned.

As Grandpa and I ate our dinner, Max and I told him about Sandra Kelly's cause of death and the weird case studies we found where people had poisoned their victims using nicotine.

"Since Connie said Sandra Kelly had an aversion to smoking, this definitely rules out her death being an accident," I said.

"Not that we ever doubted it." Max glanced from one of us to the other. "Well, I didn't."

When I got home, I gave Jazzy some wet food. She'd had dry kibble in her bowl at the shop, but she was acting as if I'd starved her for a week.

I was getting ready to take a bath, put on my pajamas, and watch television when Jason called.

"Hi, there," I said. "This is a nice surprise."

He'd been so busy with school events lately that I hadn't expected to hear from him until tomorrow.

"I have an even bigger surprise. I'm with Blake Talbot, and he wants to speak with you."

"What?" Why in the world would Blake Talbot want to talk with me? "Okay...put him on."

"We'd like to come over," Jason said. "That is, if it isn't too late."

"No. That's fine." Curiosity would've made me say that even if it was midnight rather than eight p.m.

"Are you sure? We can try for tomorrow if you'd rather not have us barge in on you tonight."

"Tonight is fine," I repeated.

After ending the call, I wondered again what Blake Talbot could possibly want with me. I was only making some costumes for the play. I had nothing to do with the budget or anything concerning the production's finances. Mr. Talbot had to know that Mrs. Berry had taken over all the administrative duties.

Fortunately, I didn't have long to wait. Jason and Mr. Talbot must've been nearby. Upon reflection, Jason had likely phoned me on the way to my house, knowing I'd agree to meet with them. Did that make me a pushover? I hoped not, but I decided I'd worry about that later. Tonight, it suited my purposes to rearrange my plans—such as they were—to accommodate a man I wanted to interrogate.

When the men arrived, Jason greeted me with a peck on the lips before introducing me to Blake Talbot.

"I've heard a lot about you, Mr. Talbot," I said.

"Please call me Blake." His eyes darted around my living room as if he was trying to ascertain what sort of person lived here. Well, the joke was on him. This had been my parents' home before they'd moved to Florida, and I'd left the house much the same. The only rooms I'd redecorated were my bedroom and the guestroom, which I'd turned into a sewing room.

"Would either of you like something to drink before we sit down?" I asked.

Both declined. Jason sat on the sofa, and I sat beside him. Blake perched on the edge of the armchair facing us.

"I realize how strange it must seem for me to ask to see you this evening," Blake began. "And before you ask, no, Jason and I were not out drinking again." He gave an uncomfortable chortle.

"I wasn't going to ask." What business was it of mine whether he and Jason had met at a bar or not?

"Oh...right. Well."

I wanted the man to quit floundering and get to the point. "Go ahead and spit it out," I prodded, smiling to soften my words.

"All right. Jason said he told you Sandy and I were working on taking down an embezzler."

"He did. I understand you believe the bookkeeper is the one stealing funds," I said.

"Right. We don't—" He sighed and ran a hand through his thinning hair. "We thought it had to be Kramer. No one else has the access he does."

"Are you sure about that?" I thought there were always checks and balances in place to ensure no one could easily steal from a school. Of course, I could be wrong.

Blake spread his hands. "He's the most likely culprit."

"Please pardon my ignorance," I said, "but I don't see how I can be of any help in this matter. I have nothing to do with the finances for the play. Mrs. Berry is in charge now. Have you spoken with her?"

"No." He lowered his eyes. "Mrs. Berry doesn't care for me very much."

"The woman was vocal in expressing her disdain for Blake's friendship with Sandy," Jason explained.

Blake nodded. "Yeah. She made it clear loudly and often. But I wondered if Sandy had discussed any of this with you?"

"No," I said. "I only met her twice—once at the school and then for lunch at the Down South Café where we discussed the costumes the day she was...found."

"I understand." Blake still didn't raise his head.

Turning to Jason, I asked, "You mentioned the band director?"

"I did," Jason confirmed. "Blake talked with him earlier today, and he said he'd go back through his ledger."

"So that's promising."

"Not really," Blake said. "He wasn't convincing. Everybody thought Sandy and I were having an affair and that I've concocted this story to explain why we were together so often...you know, now that she's gone."

"Does everybody include your wife?" I asked.

Jason gaped at me, and Blake finally looked up. Max would've been proud of me.

"Martha didn't know how much time I'd been spending with Sandy." Blake's eyes filled. "I tried to keep it from her."

He tried. Sounds like maybe he didn't succeed. I'd love to know what Martha Talbot is thinking.

As soon as Jason and Blake left, I logged onto social media and checked the message feature to see whether Max was online. She was, so I sent her a video chat request.

She accepted but didn't know quite how it was supposed to work at first. "Hello? Are you—? Oh! Yes, there you are. I can see you!" She laughed. "Do you see me?"

"I do. I'm glad you're online." I told her about my meeting with Jason and Blake Talbot.

"The wife knows," she said. "I'd bet my last sawbuck on it. You didn't happen to see a pack of gaspers on the guy, did you?"

"No, I don't believe he smokes." I recalled how he'd teared up when I'd asked about his wife. "Why do you think Blake killed Sandy?"

"I didn't say that, darling. Imagine what delicious revenge the wife could have if she killed the woman she believed to be her husband's lover and framed him for the murder." She rested her chin in her hands. "But since he doesn't smoke, it appears that bucket has a hole in it."

"Actually, Max, your theory could still hold water. I wonder if Martha Talbot is a smoker?"

Chapter Twenty-One

I'd had an idea sometime during the night, so on Tuesday morning, I went up to see Jason as soon as I'd gotten Jazzy settled.

"Hi." I smiled at him from the doorway as I watched him packing up his gear for the day.

"Hi, yourself." He walked over to me. "You look stunning."

"Thank you."

He pulled me into the studio, closed the door behind us, and gave me a proper kiss. I almost forgot what I'd gone there to tell him. Almost.

"I had an idea last night," I said. "What if Blake asked his wife to help with the play? I don't know what her strengths are, but maybe she could befriend Mrs. Berry and let her know Blake's suspicions about Kramer. It could also help save his marriage." I shrugged. "He didn't say so, but I believe he's concerned about it."

Jason nodded. "He's afraid of losing everything. He's already lost Sandra—even though they weren't having an affair, he loved her once...maybe still—and he doesn't want to lose his family." He caressed my cheek and ran his thumb over my lower lip before kissing me again. "You're wonderful, you know that?"

"I try." I nodded toward the equipment. "Where are you off to today?"

"John S. Battle High," he said. "I hope to see you later."

"I hope so too. But for now, we'd both better get to work."

I hadn't seen Max all morning. I imagined that she'd used up too much energy last night exploring the world of social media.

While I was cutting out the teacup pattern, I heard someone come into the reception area. I put down my scissors and went to the front room.

"Hi, there. Welcome to Designs on You," I said. "What can I help you find?"

The woman, who was in her mid- to late-fifties and dressed in a floor-length fur coat, said, "I want an extravagant Cleopatra costume for Halloween. I'm talking Liz Taylor in the 1963 movie with Burton." She spread her hands. "Gold cape, headdress, the whole nine yards."

"All right." I went over to the desk and got my laptop. "Let's have a seat and make sure we're on the same page."

I sat on one of the navy chairs by the window, and the Cleo wannabe sat on the other. I opened the laptop and did an image search for the Cleopatra movie starring Elizabeth Taylor. And, there she was in all her glory.

Max popped in to look over my shoulder. "Oh...Elizabeth Taylor. She's the one you compared Jason's ex—the tomato—to?"

Nodding, I turned the screen around to my customer.

"I see it," Max said. "A little. Carla isn't as pretty as this woman."

I silently agreed. The more I got to know Carla, the less attractive she became to me.

The woman I was now referring to in my mind as Cleo turned the screen back toward me. "Yes. That one right there—the dress with the one bare shoulder—that's the one I want. But I also want the gold cape and the headdress just like in the picture to the right of this one. Can you do that?"

"I can." I stood and placed the laptop back on the desk. "Let me get my notebook and tape measure."

Cleo's words stopped me before I got to the atelier. "How much is this gonna set me back? Fifty to seventy-five dollars?"

Max guffawed. "In her dreams maybe."

I turned back toward Cleo. "There's no way I can design a custom gown so inexpensively, especially not one this intricate."

Cleo gave me an exaggerated blink. "It's. A. Halloween. Costume."

It was incredibly hard for me not to throw her condescending attitude right back in her entitled face. "It's an intricately-designed and made gown. And a cape. And a headdress."

"I saw something similar on a costume site for just over forty dollars," Cleo said.

"Then I think you should probably buy it," I said.

"Well!" And with that, Cleo dramatically stood and flounced out of Designs on You.

"Now you're on the trolley!" Max exclaimed.

"Thank you." I laughed. "I'm glad I didn't waste much time on that endeavor. And I'm happy to see you. I'm guessing you had a long night."

"I was exhausted when I finally faded out of here sometime in the wee hours of the day. I'm going to have to learn to pace myself," she said. "But there are so many fascinating things on that social media thing."

Jazzy heard Max talking with me in the reception area and got out of her bed to join us.

"Hello, lovely."

The cat sat and looked up at her.

Max sighed. "I wish I could hold her."

"The fact that you can't might be the reason she loves you so much," I said. "By the way, I had a thought about Martha Talbot. I mentioned to Jason this morning that he might speak with Blake about having Martha become involved in the play. I thought it could help expose the embezzler, but it would also mean I could learn more about her."

She smiled. "Ah, Nancy Drew, we're at it again."

"Speaking of investigations, I forgot to tell you I've found more out about Dot's son, Dwight," I said. "He was an auto mechanic and married a woman named Penny Sue Delp."

"Did they have children?" she asked, leaning forward.

I nodded and felt a lump form in my throat. "Three. Two daughters and a son. Maxine, Grace, and Dwight."

"Maxine." The word emerged as a whisper. "For his sister, of course."

"And, I imagine, for his mother's beloved sister." I patted her hand, but of course, I was touching thin air.

Frank didn't accompany us to rehearsal that evening. He said he planned on staying at home in his workshop and painting the ottoman fabric. I was glad to have Grandpa to myself so we could speak freely about Max, Sandra Kelly's murder, and anything else that happened to cross our minds.

When we parked at the school, I spotted Blake Talbot standing by the door talking with a woman. She was slightly plump, had dark hair, and wore sunglasses. I realized they were standing outside because she was smoking. A chill snaked down my spine.

I exchanged a glance with Grandpa before we walked toward the door.

"Mrs. Talbot, I assume?" he said under his breath.

"That's my guess."

When we got to the door, I saw that the woman wasn't smoking but, in fact, vaping. I wasn't sure what the difference was except I knew vaping involved electronic cigarettes.

"Amanda." Blake greeted me with a broad smile. "I'd like you to meet my wife, Martha."

"It's a pleasure to meet you," I said. "This is my grandfather Dave Tucker. He's also helping out with the production."

"Don't worry—I'm not making dresses," Grandpa said. "I'm just helping with the sets."

Since Martha hadn't made an effort to speak to us yet, Blake filled in the gap. "Sweetie, Amanda is Jason's girl. Remember? I told you about her."

"Yeah. Sure." She puffed on her vape pen, which looked a lot like a USB drive.

He tried again but lowered his voice this time. "It was Amanda's idea to have you get involved with the play so that you can tell Mrs. Berry you suspect Kramer of embezzling."

"Joy," Martha said flatly.

"We'd better get inside," I told Grandpa. "Blake, nice seeing you again. And, Martha..." I didn't want to say it was a pleasure meeting her because it certainly hadn't been. "See you in the auditorium, I guess."

Once the door had closed behind us and he felt confident we were out of earshot, Grandpa said, "Well, Martha is a pure delight."

"Isn't she though?"

Chapter Twenty-Two

I met up with Zoe in the auditorium. I still needed to get measurements for the wardrobe, clock, and candlestick.

"Would you mind gathering up the actors for our remaining costumes?" I asked. "After tonight, I should be out of your hair for a while."

"Why's that?"

"Well, I thought I could work on the costumes at my shop in the evenings and get them finished quicker." I took out the notepad where I was keeping my measurements and then took a pen from the pocket of my tote.

"But..." Zoe hesitated. Looking back, I realized she was coming up with an excuse for me to have to be there at the school. "But won't you need to be here if your volunteers have questions? And what if an actor gets sick or something, and you have to make last-minute adjustments to your measurements? Wouldn't it be better to do that before you make the costume?"

"Of course." I nodded. "You're right. I should be here for rehearsals. I can always work on the costumes when I get home."

She let out a breath. "I mean, do whatever you want. I'm only trying to save you some extra work."

"Thanks. So, who do we have first?"

"How about the wardrobe?" she asked. "She's cool. You'll like her."

I hadn't disliked any of the kids yet, but I didn't point that fact out to Zoe. While I was waiting for Zoe to return with the wardrobe, I glanced over at a corner of the room where a table had been knocked sideways. A pile of papers, notebooks, and folders were scattered about on the floor. My best guess was that Biscuit or Gravy had bumped the table yesterday when they were conducting their wild rumpus.

I went over to straighten up the mess and put the items back on the table. As I picked up the notebooks, I noticed that one was actually a planner. I opened the front cover and saw that it was Sandra Kelly's planner. Could there be a clue in here as to who might've wanted her dead?

I thumbed through the book to the week before Sandra's murder.

"Here we are!" Zoe called.

I closed the planner and slipped it into my tote before going over to meet the wardrobe.

"Ms. Tucker, this is Priscilla. Priscilla, Ms. Tucker." Zoe grinned. "When Ms. Tucker has her cat with her, she reminds me of a Bond villain, but she's pretty cool."

"Hi, Priscilla," I said before lowering my voice to a stage whisper. "Don't tell Zoe, but I am a Bond villain."

Priscilla giggled. "Don't tell Zoe, but I'm a Bond villain in training. I've been working on my lair."

"Nice!" I smiled.

Zoe rolled her eyes. "Weirdos."

"Takes one to know one," Priscilla said.

Grandpa told me on the way home that Martha had been assigned to help him and Ford with the sets.

"Lucky you." I playfully elbowed him in the ribs. "Was she as sweet as I'd expect her to be, given that stellar first impression?"

He waffled his hand. "She wasn't overly friendly, but she was friendlier than she'd been outside. She did go out and take several smoke breaks—said her sister Jessica got her hooked on those vape things."

"I thought people weren't allowed to smoke on school property."

Shrugging, he said, "Maybe that doesn't apply to vaping. I have no idea."

I decided to confess. "I found Sandra's planner in the auditorium. I'm going to look through the planner tonight to see if I can find any clues as to who murdered her."

"And then tomorrow first thing, you'll turn it over to Detective Cranston?" he asked.

"Of course, I will!"

Jason stopped by with a gorgeous white mum in a green and gold planter. "The John S. Battle horticulturist club was selling these, and I thought you might like one for your front porch."

"It's beautiful. Thank you." I asked if he'd like something to eat or drink.

"As much as I'd love to stay awhile, I need to get home," he said. "Oh, hey, did you get to meet Blake's wife today?"

"Um...yeah."

He chuckled at the expression on my face which I can only imagine betrayed what I'd thought about Martha Talbot.

"Have you met her?" I asked.

"Only once, and she didn't go out of her way to be nice." His laughter bubbled up again. "I imagine she'd be even more unfriendly toward a beautiful woman."

I shook my head. "Not every woman is a rival for her husband's attention."

"True, but Blake broke the woman's trust once." His smile faded. "And if you can't trust your spouse, who can you trust?"

I remembered what Max had said about a wife's revenge and had to repress a shudder. After Jason had left, I did an online search for nicotine and vaping. I found that e-cigarettes and other vaping devices deliver as much nicotine—if not more—than a regular cigarette. So, Martha could have theoretically poisoned Sandra Kelly with nicotine. But how?

You know how sometimes you do something else to get your mind off a problem, and then you come up with a solution to the problem while you're doing the other thing? That's what I hoped would happen while I looked through Sandra Kelly's planner. Maybe I'd find something to connect Sandra and Martha—well, other than the obvious connection of Blake.

I started with the day of the murder. Sandra had her lunch with me at the Down South Café on her schedule, and she had IBS – Karen at three o'clock, and then rehearsal at four-thirty that day.

Hmm...IBS? What's that?

The only thing I could come up with was irritable bowel syndrome, so I did a search for IBS acronyms. I found too many to count, including intellectual belittling syndrome, Institute of Behavioral Science, and International Builders' Show. When I searched for IBS – Karen, I found lots of articles on how women named Karen learned to live with their irritable bowel syndrome.

I blew out a breath. Surely to goodness, Sandra Kelly hadn't been planning to meet with Karen, whose main defining feature was that she had irritable bowel syndrome. There simply had to be a more sensible explanation.

Going backward though Sandra's planner, I found where she'd made a note to call Child Protective Services two days prior to her death. Given what she'd told me about Zoe's homelife, I was guessing Sandra had called—or had planned to call—CPS about Maggie Flannagan. Had she called? If so, had she talked with Zoe's mother before making the call?

I flipped through the pages looking for a meeting with Maggie Flannagan, but I didn't find anything. It was possible they'd met but that Sandra had neglected to put it on her schedule, but I felt that was unlikely given how meticulous she'd been about documenting everything else. There were no further entries about CPS either. Who would know whether Sandra Kelly had contacted CPS or not? I didn't want to call the agency myself if Sandra had realized she was making a mistake and hadn't called. And if she had, then surely CPS was investigating.

Amid the yoga classes, the nail appointments, and the inspirational quotes, there were lots of notations that simply had the word "Blake" or the initials "BT." I had to wonder if the two of them really were having an affair. After all, Sandra's marriage had supposedly ended because of Blake Talbot. Had she still been in love with Blake when she died? Had her love for him been the reason she'd died?

Chapter Twenty-Three

First thing Wednesday morning, Diana Kramer came in to pick up the suit I was holding for her.

"I'm glad you're able to get it sooner than you'd thought," I said.

With a wide grin, she said, "Me too. Fergus and I came into an unexpected little windfall."

"That's terrific."

She hugged the garment bag containing the suit to her chest. "I know. I don't normally indulge myself like this, but I absolutely love this suit."

"So do I, and it fits you like a custom-made piece."

"If anybody asks, it was." She winked. Putting the garment bag down long enough to pay me, she saw the yellow dress I was making for *Beauty and the Beast*. "I hope you're getting paid for your work for Winter Garden High. Don't let those people take advantage of you. Honestly, if you give an inch, they'll take two yards."

I smiled. "I am getting paid, but mostly, this is good for publicity. My shop is relatively new here, and I'm still getting established."

"Well, I'll certainly spread the word at the salon. I gave you a card, didn't I?"

"You did," I said. "Indulgences Beauty Salon." As soon as I'd said it, something clicked within my brain. Indulgences Beauty Salon—IBS. "Diana, was Sandra Kelly a client at your salon?"

"She wasn't one of my clients, but she might have seen one of the other stylists."

"How about Karen? Is there someone by that name who works with you?"

She nodded. "Yeah, we have a Karen. Why?"

"Sandra mentioned her." She did mention her in her planner. "And her hair was beautifully highlighted." That was also true.

"If you're considering highlights, I'm your gal." Diana walked over and looked more closely at my hair. "I could give you some lovely highlights and lowlights to really give your hair dimension and pop."

Naturally, Max chose that moment to "pop" in and say, "Know what else would give your hair some pop? Poking your finger into an electrical outlet."

I clamped my lips together firmly. I waited out my urge to laugh before speaking again. "I'm still thinking about it."

"Don't be such a Nervous Nellie," Diana said. "When you decide to pull that trigger, give me a call. Me—not Karen. She's not as experienced as I am."

I thanked her, and she took her suit and left.

"My, my, my. She's awfully full of herself." Max pointed her index finger and thumb at me. "Are you going to pull that trigger?"

"No. I believe my hair has enough dimension and pop as is."

"Me too, darling. Were you merely chatting her up? Or was there a reason for your asking about Karen?"

I told Max about finding Sandra's planner and that an appointment with Karen from IBS was scheduled for the last afternoon of her life.

"Ah, so we need to talk with Karen."

"Yes, we do," I said. "Women often confide in their hairdressers, you know. Maybe Karen can tell me something about how Sandra was feeling or what she had on her mind that day."

Retrieving Diana's business card from my desk drawer, I called Indulgences Beauty Salon. I got the answering machine. Either the business was closed on Wednesdays, or it wasn't open early in the day.

"Hi," I said. "This message is for Karen." I left my name and number and asked that Karen call me at her earliest convenience.

"And now we wait," Max said. "I do despise waiting."

Before I could commiserate with Max, Trish Oakes walked into Designs on You. She had her hair up in a bun today, making her angular features appear even sharper than usual.

"Good morning, Amanda. I'm talking with everyone this morning to find out what we're doing to frighten prospective vendors away from leasing the vacant space upstairs.

"I'm haunting the joint," Max said.

I covered my laugh with a coughing fit. "Excuse me."

"Tell her about Carla." Max floated in front of me with her arms up over her head, fingers wagging.

That broke me, and I couldn't hide that bubble of laughter.

"What's so funny?" Ms. Oakes demanded.

"It's just that Carla, the massage therapist, seemed to believe there was something supernatural going on at Shops on Main," I said.

"Don't be ridiculous. Carla is the only person who has given me a valid reason for not leasing the space. The stairs created a mobility issue for some of her patients." She sniffed. "Not that it matters to me, but she found what appears to be a charming space in Lebanon."

Barely containing my delight that Carla had opened her business at least half an hour's drive away, I asked, "What about Mr. Bare?"

"What about him?" Ms. Oakes narrowed her eyes. "Did you say something disparaging to him?"

"Of course not. You were with me when I met him," I reminded. "You heard everything I said to him. And even though I found him to be an eccentric, I thought he might've been a fun addition to the Shops on Main family. What reason did he give for turning down the space?"

"He and the painter both said they thought the rent was too high."

I flipped my palms. "There you go. Have you thought about lowering the rent for that space?"

"No, I have not! If I lower the rent for one, the rest of you will expect me to lower your rent as well. Anyway, it's utter nonsense. The rent is perfectly reasonable." Raising an index finger, she said,

"Someone in this building is being off-putting to new prospects, and I'm going to find out who it is."

"I told you, I'm haunting the joint!" Max shouted at Ms. Oakes' retreating back. "What else can I do? She won't listen."

"She wouldn't listen to me either, and I know she could hear me," I said. "No one is being mean to prospective vendors." I grinned. "Well, not to all of them."

"Lebanon is far away from Jason's studio," Max singsonged.

"I know." I gave her a double thumbs up. "Thank you for your help in making that happen."

"You are ever so welcome, but it was nothing. Nothing I didn't enjoy to the fullest."

Before we could further gloat over Carla's finding a location out of town, Frank came into the shop with the fabric he'd painted for the *Beauty and the Beast* ottoman.

"Look what I've got," he said, holding it up in front of him.

"Oh, my goodness. That's incredible." I quickly cleared off a space on the worktable so he could spread it out.

The ivory fabric had been filled with muted green, purple, orange, and gold paisleys, along with light blue accent dots and swirls.

"Jeepers!" Max eased closer. "I'd love to have a dress made of this."

Frank rubbed his arms. "I just got a chill."

Smiling slightly, I said, "Me too." I looked at the cloth for a long moment. "Frank, we can't use this."

"Why not? I worked hard on it."

"That's precisely why we can't use it." I gently ran my hand over one of the paisleys. "You could sell this fabric and make a heck of a lot more money than what you'll get from the school."

"But I didn't make it to sell—I made it specifically to be used in the play." He sounded hurt.

"I know." I sighed. "What if we ask for it back after the play so we could carefully deconstruct the costume and you could repurpose the fabric? I mean—do you realize what an incredible work of art this is?"

He blushed as he drew himself up to his full height. "I'm fairly proud of it, sure, but...you know...I made it for the kids."

"I'll talk with Mrs. Berry this afternoon and ask if we can have the ottoman costume back once the play is over."

"All right," he said. "Oh, by the way, I won't be needing a ride today. I talked so much about the play that Ella wants to help out too. She's coming with me."

"He seems happy about that," Max mused as Frank left the room.

"He does, doesn't he?" I smiled. "Good." I hoped it would last.

Chapter Twenty-Four

I spent the afternoon finishing the Belle dress. With Kristen's parents at least partially footing the bill for the costumes, I thought I should get her gown completed first and make sure she was happy with it. I was pleased with it.

Putting the gown on the dress form, I added rosettes to the bodice.

Max stood behind the dress form and spread her arms, pretending she was wearing the gown. "This makes me feel like a princess. I want to twirl around and sing that sappy tune from the movie—you know the one—something about 'old tails.'" She began to hum.

I recognized the movie's main theme song from the ballroom scene. "Let's hope Kristen is as pleased with the dress as you are."

After putting the final touches on the gown, I transferred it to a garment bag. "What do you plan to do this evening?"

"I'm listening to that wonderful audiobook you downloaded for me," she said. "And as I listen to that, I thought I might try to find more information on Dot's son, Dwight. Any clues where I should start?"

I gave her the name of the genealogy site I'd used.

She looked pensive. "Do you think he might still be alive?"

Doing a quick calculation in my head—and trying to remember the year of Dwight's birth—I determined him to be in his early eighties. "It's possible. If I'm remembering his date of birth correctly, he'd be eighty-one."

"So...pretty old." She turned down the corners of her mouth. "But people these days live longer than we did. You know, unless they tumble headfirst down the stairs."

"Good luck." I gathered up the dress, Jazzy, and my tote bag and headed out.

Jazzy and I were having dinner with Grandpa before going to the school. He'd promised it would be ready when we got there. And since I'd only had a granola bar for lunch, I was thoroughly looking forward to dinner.

With our bellies full of barbecue chicken and potato salad, Grandpa and I strolled into Winter Garden High. I don't know about Grandpa, but I was shocked to find Ella Peterman and Martha Talbot talking and laughing in the hall.

"Hi, Ella," I said. "I'm happy you're joining us."

"I couldn't let Frank have all the fun." She turned toward her companion. "Martha, do you know Amanda and Dave?"

Martha nodded. "Yes, I met them both yesterday. Good to see you again."

"I'm looking forward to seeing that masterpiece Frank created," Grandpa told Ella. "Amanda says it's beautiful."

Ella beamed. "It is. He really outdid himself."

"That reminds me—I need to have a word with Mrs. Berry." I excused myself and went to find the woman. She was in the auditorium in the center of the fifth row of seats.

"Project!" she called to the actors onstage. "Your audience needs to be able to hear you in the back row!"

"Hi, Mrs. Berry. May I have a word?"

"Of course, Ms. Tucker." She nodded at the seat next to her.

Making my way past the other seats, I realized I'd have been wise to put my things in my work area before seeking out Mrs. Berry. "I won't take but a moment of your time, but I wonder if it would be possible to reclaim the ottoman costume once the play is over."

She gave me an appraising look but said nothing.

"Mr. Peterman hand painted the fabric, and it's gorgeous," I continued. "I'd like to deconstruct the costume following its use in the production so that he may repurpose the fabric."

"As the Holbrooks are subsidizing the costumes, they'll be deciding what to do with them," she said.

I thanked her and went on to my allotted space backstage.

Zoe was there already. "Hi." What's in the bag?"

"Belle's dress." I removed the dress from the garment bag and hung it up.

"Whoa..." Zoe touched the material lightly. "That's gorgeous."

"Thank you."

"Is that my dress?" Kristen asked, rushing over to us. She squealed, grabbed the dress, and held it to her front. "I love it! It's just the way we designed it."

"Yep." We had worked awfully hard on this dress.

"I'm going to try it on." She went behind the screen we'd put up for actors' privacy and slipped into the dress. She called to have me zip it up, and then she hurried off, calling over her shoulder, "I'm going to show Connor!"

"And there went Hurricane Kristen," Zoe said.

I grinned. "I'm glad she likes the dress."

"I'm glad you're here. I mean, I know it would be a lot easier for you to work from your shop, but—" She shrugged. "I like having you here. Mrs. Berry is so bossy and mean. It's more fun when you're around."

"Thanks. Remember, though, Mrs. Berry didn't want Ms. Kelly's job. And, if it weren't for her, the play wouldn't be happening."

"Yeah, yeah. You did your due diligence in not letting me gripe about the old lady."

Laughing, I said, "Okay. Between us, I'm glad I'm your favorite."

"You're everybody's favorite." She looked down at her hands. "About my mom... I hope you didn't get the wrong impression of my her."

I hoped I didn't get the right impression of the woman. "I realize being a single mom can't be easy."

"It's not," Zoe said. "Mom has a lot on her."

To dispel the uncomfortable silence that fell between us, I said, "I brought a portable sewing machine with me so I can work on some of the simpler costumes here. Would you like to learn how to sew?"

"Really?" She moved closer. "You'll teach me?"

"Sure. You and I are going to make the candlestick costume this afternoon."

Kristen returned and took the dress back off so I could hang it up.

"Put it back in the garment bag," she said. "I'm taking it home with me."

I did as she asked. "Could you please have your mom give me a call? I want to talk with her about the ottoman costume."

"Sure. Or you could talk with her when she comes to pick me up after rehearsal." She took the garment bag from me. "My car is getting new tires today, so Mom brought me to school."

"All right," I said. "I'll look forward to talking with her then."

"I'll come get you and the dress before I leave." With a wave, she was gone.

"Have you ever met Kristen's mom?" I asked Zoe.

She shook her head but continued concentrating on the seam she was sewing. "I imagine she's just an older version of Kristen."

Zoe was pretty much right on the money. Dr. Holbrook was very much an older version of her daughter.

After rehearsal, Kristen directed me toward her mother's black Mercedes in the parking lot. "Mom, wait until you see my Belle dress."

"I can hardly wait." Dr. Holbrook got out of the car and smiled at her daughter before turning back to me. "Thank you for your hard work."

"I enjoy it. Thank you for your patronage," I said. "I wanted to ask you what you plan to do with the costumes after the play."

"Most of them will be donated to a local children's theater group. Of course, we'll hang on to Kristen's 'Belle' gown. Why?"

I explained that Frank Peterman had put quite a bit of hard work into the fabric for the ottoman costume. "I was going to buy textile fabric, but he insisted on hand painting the fabric to match the décor of the set."

Dr. Holbrook put an elegantly manicured hand to her chest. "How exquisite!"

"It really is. I wondered if there would be any way we could have the ottoman costume back so it could be carefully deconstructed so Mr. Peterman can repurpose the fabric."

"Oh, of course, we can do that," she said. "I realize you're not getting paid enough for your time and expertise. Giving Mr. Peterman the ottoman is the least we can do. We'll be happy to have you keep any of the other costumes you're particularly attached to."

"No, I'm fine with the rest of them being donated." I noticed Dr. Holbrook's gaze shift to something behind me and turned to see Martha Talbot coming out of the school.

"Who is that?" Dr. Holbrook asked. "She looks familiar."

"Her name is Martha Talbot," I said.

"Yeah, Mom. She's the math teacher's wife."

"Oh...right." She arched a brow. "Now I remember seeing her before. Poor woman."

"You'd better believe poor woman," Kristen said. "Mr. Talbot is the one who was having the fling with Ms. Kelly."

"Yes, I know." Dr. Holbrook looked back at me. "I was going to have Sandra Kelly fired—and the math teacher as well. But now Ms. Kelly is dead, and after seeing Mrs. Talbot here helping with the play, I'm glad I didn't have her husband dismissed. After all, poor Mrs. Talbot is suffering enough without her family losing their main source of income." She scrunched up her face to the extent the Botox would allow. "She doesn't work, does she?"

"I have no idea," I said. "I've only spoken to her in passing."

Keeping my smile plastered firmly in place, I thought that if Blake Talbot knew what was good for him, he'd get out of Winter Garden High School as soon as possible. He wasn't well-liked at the school— that was putting it mildly—and he needed to leave before someone else like Dr. Holbrook decided she didn't care whether or not his family lost their primary source of income. Even if he had to take a job in another state, it would have to be better than working at this school.

"Do you know Fergus Kramer?" I asked Dr. Holbrook.

"Yes, our family has known Ferg for ages. Why?"

"It's just that he and Ms. Kelly appeared to be having an argument the first evening I came here about the play. I thought maybe they were disagreeing about how production funds were being allocated."

"I doubt that," Dr. Holbrook said. "Sandra Kelly had nothing to do with the play's budget. All of that is being overseen by Ferg and me. I mean, as the production's main benefactors, my husband and I felt we should have a say in how the funds are spent." She smiled at Kristen. "Making sure our daughter's senior play is a success rather than looking like something the Little Rascals would throw together in a barn is crucial to her father and me."

"I understand completely." Smiling at both of them, I said goodnight and went in search of Grandpa. I couldn't help wondering what would happen to poor Kristen if there ever came a time when her parents were unable to pave the way for her.

Chapter Twenty-Five

I caught up to Grandpa, who was standing with Frank and Ella by their van chatting. Martha Talbot was with them too.

"Good news, Frank," I said. "After the play, the ottoman costume is all yours."

With a broad smile, he thanked me. "That is good news."

"What are you going to do with it?" Martha asked.

"I'm not sure. I'll have to give that some thought." He looked at Ella to see if she had any suggestions.

"Maybe we can find a way to display it at Everything Paper with a photo of the actor wearing the finished costume." She patted his arm. "I'm so proud of you."

I was seeing a whole new side to Frank and Ella. I wondered if perhaps his art was what had drawn her to him in the first place and then life, making a living, providing for the two of them got in the way and he drifted away from more ambitious work. It was as if Frank's rekindling of his artistic passion had re-minded her of the man she'd fallen in love with.

"Mrs. Berry had me ask Dr. Holbrook about the costume, since the Holbrooks are in large part fund-ing the production." I gave Martha a pointed look. "Dr. Holbrook said she'd known 'Ferg' Kramer for years and that she and her husband were keeping tabs on how the money is being allocated."

After explaining to Frank and Ella that Blake be-lieves someone—most likely Mr. Kramer—is taking money from various school accounts, Martha said, "I typically take people I trust at their word and don't follow up with them too closely. If Dr. and Judge Holbrook have been friends with Mr. Kramer for a long time, they might not be watching over his ac-tions too judiciously."

"True," I said, "but I don't think Dr. Holbrook would be amenable to auditing the production's books to make sure her friend isn't embezzling."

Martha nodded. "I believe Blake is on a wild goose chase and that he should abandon this entire mess."

Although I tended to agree with her, at least, to an extent, I wisely didn't offer my opinion on the subject.

Driving back to his house, Grandpa warned me to tread carefully where the Holbrooks were concerned.

"Kristen has already been a wonderful customer for you, and prom season hasn't even rolled around yet this year."

"I know, but I don't want Frank Kramer to continue stealing from the school."

"How do you know he is stealing from the school?" he asked. "You're going on the word of someone who is trying to rebuild his reputation. What better way to do that than to take down someone else for something the school will hopefully consider worse than what Blake himself has been accused of doing?"

"That's an excellent point." I paused. "But Diana Kramer, Fergus Kramer's wife, came into Designs on You today and picked up a suit I was to hold for her until the week before Thanksgiving. She picked it up early, saying they came into a windfall."

"You're jumping to conclusions, Pup. I picked up some extra money this past weekend at the farmers' market. Had I bought a suit today, would you have wondered where I got the money for it?"

"Of course not, but—" He was right. I didn't know where Diana Kramer got the money for the suit. "You're right."

As I drove home with Jazzy, I thought about what Grandpa had said earlier. The man made a lot of sense. I shouldn't be so willing to believe what others wanted me to believe, especially not without proof. Because Blake Talbot was Jason's friend, I'd been willing—even eager—to believe that the rumors of his current affair with Sandra Kelly had been false and that the two of them had really been trying to find evidence that either Fergus Kramer or someone else was defrauding the school.

And even if that was truly what they'd been doing when they left their classrooms unattended, that was no excuse for their neglecting their students. By the time, I got to my house, I was upset with myself for becoming an unwitting pawn for Blake Talbot. I even felt as if I owed Fergus Kramer an apology.

I'd never heard back from Karen of Indulgences Beauty Salon. Maybe sometime tomorrow I could go by the salon and talk with her and also make an appointment with Diana Kramer. I didn't want highlights or lowlights, but I could let her give my hair a trim.

Max wasn't around when I got to work the next morning, and I wondered how late she'd been online the night before. I'd been tired when I'd gotten home and had spent the evening reading a magazine article about honeybees. As interesting as it was—no, really—I'd dozed off.

I'd intended to see if Max was online after I'd taken my bath and propped up in the bed to read, but I'd decided to read the article first. Oh, well...

I was hoping she'd be here to tell me if she'd learned more about Dot's family. As I worked on a mask for the clock costume, I thought about how strange it must feel to be Max. She had been alive—or, rather dead... No. She'd been around for over a century, dead longer than alive, had seen so many people come and go, and was tethered to this property.

There was a rapid rap on the atelier door, and Connie came in. "Good morning. What are you doing?"

I showed her the white, half-face mask and explained that it was for the clock costume. "I want to take one of these masks I bought at a party supply shop and turn it into half a clock face. I'm guessing we can use eyeliner to paint additional numbers on the actor's face." I handed the mask to Connie. "Here's my dilemma. I want to be able to have moveable hands on the mask without it irritating the actor's nose."

She chuckled. "That would be terrible if this mask made the kid sneeze right in the middle of the performance." She turned the mask over to examine the back. "How was rehearsal last night?"

"It was fine. When are the middle schoolers expected to be back?"

"We'll be there tomorrow night," she said. When I groaned, she asked, "Are they that bad?"

"No, but if the middle schoolers are there, I'm guessing Joey will be there too." I shook my head. "As adorable as that child is, I hope he'll either leave his ferrets at home or else bring them in something more escape-proof than his backpack."

"Oh, wow. I'd forgotten all about Joey's ferrets."

"They made quite a splash when I measured Joey for his costume the other evening. One even wound up in Kristen Holbrook's bra." After we shared a laugh over that, I asked, "Do you the Holbrook family?"

"Not terribly well, although they have a solid reputation for being the crème de la crème of Abingdon society. Why?"

"As crazy as this sounds, I feel almost as sorry for Kristen as I do for Zoe Flannagan," I said.

"The stage manager?"

I nodded. "From the little I've seen Dr. Holbrook interacting with her daughter, I can't help but wonder how much of what she does is actually for Kristen rather than for herself."

"Both Kristen and Zoe need good adult friends they can count on," she said. "That's one reason so many of the students loved Sandy—they could comfortably confide in her, knowing she'd listen and that she'd always do whatever she could to help." She sighed. "I'd better get my tea and go back to Delightful Home. If I think of anything with regard to the clock hands, I'll let you know."

"Thanks!"

Her comment about Sandra Kelly being such a good friend to her students made me remember what

Grandpa said about people showing you what they wanted you to see. While I realized people were seldom morally black or white, I wondered which shade of gray most accurately depicted Sandra Kelly.

At lunchtime, I put a note on the reception room door, locked both entrances to Designs on You, and drove to the Indulgences Beauty Salon. I had Sandra's planner in my tote to drop off to Detective Cranston before I returned to work.

The salon might've been closed or slow on Wednesday—given that no one had returned my call—but it was flourishing today. I parked and walked inside to be assailed by the mixed scents of ammonia, hairspray, and coffee.

The stylist whose station was closest to the door said, "Hi. Do you have an appointment?"

"No, but I'd like to make one." I looked around but didn't see Diana. "Is Karen here?"

"I'm Karen."

The diminutive, cotton-haired woman in the salon chair said, "I'll vouch for her. Karen's the best of the bunch."

"Thank you, Mrs. Hawkins."

Smiling, I said, "I'm Amanda. I'm the one who left the message for you yesterday."

Karen frowned. "I didn't get any messages yesterday."

"I left it on the machine?"

Rolling her eyes, Karen said, "That's not always reliable. Whoever gets here first typically gets them, and they don't always pass the messages along. What do you need done?"

"I actually wanted to ask you about an appointment you had last Thursday."

"I was out sick on Thursday, and the other stylists divvied up my appointments." She scowled around the room at the other stylists before returning her attention to me. "Did somebody screw up on one of my customers? I knew I should've rescheduled all my appointments, but I felt too lousy to fool with it."

Holding up both hands, I said, "No, no! Nothing like that. In fact, I was really impressed with my friend's hair and wondered who did it that afternoon. Sandra Kelly?"

"I don't know who did Sandy's hair on Thursday, but I can probably find out for you." She narrowed her eyes. "You saw Sandy before she died then?"

I gulped. "We grabbed a bite to eat. I'm helping out with the play."

"Right."

"What play?" Karen's client asked. "I enjoy plays."

"I think you'd like this one then," I said. "It's the Winter Garden High School production of *Beauty and the Beast*. The students are doing a wonderful job, and they're even incorporating students from the middle school and one elementary classman for roles." I was babbling. I needed to stop babbling. But Karen was giving me the side-eye and making me feel uncomfortable.

"That sounds like such fun," Mrs. Hawkins said. "Don't you think so, Karen?"

"Yeah. Sounds great."

"I'd better go. I need to get back to work." I gave her a tight smile. "I'll call later for an appointment."

Karen leveled a gaze at me that clearly said, We both know you won't be calling.

And she was right. Even though what I'd told her was technically true—Sandra Kelly and I did grab a bite together on Thursday—Karen was suspicious of me now and had no intention of telling me who'd seen Sandra on Thursday. Besides, I didn't really need a trim. And when I did, I preferred to go to my usual stylist. Sorry, Diana.

I left the building and saw Diana and Fergus Kramer in the parking lot. I waved to her before leaving.

Upon arriving at the police station, I was informed by the desk clerk that Detective Cranston was at lunch. I asked for a notepad and a pen. The clerk pushed them across the counter to me.

I wrote Detective Cranston the following note:

I found Sandra Kelly's planner in the auditorium and thought you might want to take a look at it. I thumbed through it and found a notation that read 'IBS-Karen' for the day Sandra died. I did a little investigating and learned that IBS stands for Indulgences Beauty Salon. Karen, the stylist Sandra was scheduled to see, was sick that day but was unwilling to tell me who'd taken the appointment. Hopefully, she'll be more forthcoming with you about Sandra's frame of mind that afternoon. Please call me if you have any questions or concerns I may be able to address. – Amanda Tucker

I took the planner from my tote, put it with the note, and left. I had a feeling Detective Cranston

wasn't going to be terribly pleased with my investigating.

Chapter Twenty-Six

I dropped my granola bar wrapper into the trash can in the kitchen and grabbed a bottle of water from the refrigerator. I was already thinking about dinner—and acknowledging the fact that I needed to start having a more substantial lunch if I wanted to avoid being ravenous every afternoon.

Max was perched on the filing cabinet in the atelier. "I found him!"

"Found who?" I asked.

"Dwight. My nephew. I found him on social media. Isn't that marvelous?"

"It is!" It was, wasn't it? I moved closer to her and lowered my voice. "You didn't tell him who you were, did you?"

"No, I thought about it, but I didn't want the poor guy to think I was crackers."

"People would've thought he was the crazy one if he told anyone he was talking to his dead aunt on social media." I widened my eyes. "Did you video chat?"

"We were going to, but he couldn't figure out how to do it, so we type-chatted."

I managed not to heave a sigh of relief. Who knew what repercussions there would be if an elderly man was talking with a flapper who was the ghost of his aunt? "Who did you say you were?"

She grinned. "I told him my mother was a friend of his mother. Isn't that clever? Plus, it's the truth."

Nodding, I rolled a chair over so I could sit. "And?"

"And we chatted for a long time. He's lived here in Abingdon all his life. Isn't that great? I wonder if he's ever been in this house. Do you think I've ever seen him?" She didn't wait for my response. "He has four grandchildren and one great-grandchild. I wish I could meet them too." She frowned slightly. "But I believe he's in a home for the aged and that he might have some dementia."

"Why do you say that?"

"Well, at one point, he began calling me 'Penny' and finally said he had to get off the phone before he got into trouble with his mom."

"That's sad," I said. "Did he look like Dot?"

"Are you asking me if my sister—who I remember as a beautiful sixteen-year-old bears any resemblance to an old man?" she asked, scrunching up her nose.

"No. I'm asking if Dot's son bore any resemblance to her. You saw his photo, didn't you?"

"Not well enough to tell whether or not he looked like Dot."

"You didn't scroll through his photos?" I asked. "I'd have thought maybe he'd have one of him when he was younger—even perhaps one of him and Dot."

"Go get him."

Feeling certain I'd misunderstood her, I retrieved my laptop. As I was logging into my social media account, she said, "No, not that. I want you to go get Dwight and bring him here."

I gaped at her. "I can't do that."

"Why not?"

"Nursing homes frown on residents being kidnapped by strangers. The police don't care for the practice either." I could see myself trying to explain that one to Detective Cranston. Oh, hey, well, my friend the ghost wanted to meet her nephew in person, and since she's tethered to Shops on Main...

"Oh, pooh on the coppers."

"Easy for you to say—you wouldn't be the one banging your tin cup on the bars of a jail cell," I said.

"Isn't there anything you can do?" she wailed.

I hated seeing her look so dejected. "How about this? We'll find out which nursing home Dwight is staying in, and I'll go talk with him. I'll see if he has any photos there, and if he does, I'll ask if I can take pictures of them with my phone so you can see them."

"Thank you," she said.

I merely smiled and resolved to talk to Grandpa about this situation as soon as I could without Max hearing.

The quick tap that I recognized as Connie's knock sounded, and I was relieved she'd arrived to put an end to this conversation—at least, for now.

"Come on in!" I called.

"I've been thinking about your mask." She pushed the door closed behind her and brought out some strips of Velcro®. "I think this will work. Don't you?"

"Let's see." I picked up the mask and placed one side of the strip to jut from under the mask at the tip of the nose. Taping it in place, I put the mask on my face to ensure that I could breathe and that my vision wouldn't be obstructed. "If the hands will attach to this, I think it will work."

"If you put the grabby side at the nose and make the hands out of the other strip, do you think that would work?" Connie asked.

"I do."

She and I worked on the mask until we had hands that would work and wouldn't aggravate the actor's face.

I smiled in triumph. "I'll get the superglue. And while the grabby Velcro® strip dries, I can finish the body of the costume."

"Glad I could help." She jerked her head toward the hall. "I'd better get back."

By the time Connie left, Max had disappeared.

I'd finished up the clock costume and was cutting out the wardrobe when Detective Cranston strolled into Designs on You and leaned against the doorframe between the reception area and the atelier. "I got your note."

"Why do I get the impression you aren't pleased about that?" I asked, laying aside my scissors.

"You should've turned Sandra Kelly's planner in to me as soon as you found it."

"It was late, and I wanted to go home, Detective. Besides, didn't I help you out by deciphering that IBS notation?"

He arched a brow. "You don't believe I could've figured that out on my own?"

"I'm positive you could have," I said. "But since you didn't have to, it saved you some time." I inclined my head. "Would you like some coffee?"

"No, thank you." He came on into the atelier. "What in the world are you making?"

"A wardrobe costume—for *Beauty and the Beast.*"

Giving a rumble of amusement, he asked, "You don't do anything halfway, do you?"

"No, sir, not if I can help it. About the beauty salon, did it turn up any good leads?"

"None of the other stylists would admit to doing Sandra Kelly's hair that afternoon," he said, "and there was nothing on the books that proved she was even there. Maybe she canceled since her regular stylist was busy."

"I guess that's possible..."

"But you don't think so, do you?" he asked, rolling his eyes.

I shrugged. "It's awfully coincidental. I remember Connie saying Sandra's scalp was bleeding and that clumps of her hair had fallen out."

"That doesn't prove she went to the salon," he said. "She could've gotten some product at the grocery store to touch up her hair until she could get in to see her regular gal."

"A product with nicotine in it?" I paused for effect. "But you're right. I'm probably making too much of it. Did the medical examiner ever say how the poison was administered to Sandra Kelly?"

"How about you let me worry about that, and you concentrate on making your wardrobe costume?"

Chapter Twenty-Seven

As Grandpa drove us to Winter Garden High later that afternoon, I told him all about Max and Dwight.

"Thank goodness he couldn't figure out how to video chat," I said. "Either he'd have thought she was hiding somewhere out of the frame, or he'd have seen her. I don't know which would have been worse."

"If he's in a nursing home, I'll tell you which would be worse—Dwight sitting at the computer talking with someone only he could see and hear." He gave a low whistle. "If he's already showing signs of dementia like Max said, the nursing home staff would believe him to be completely off his rocker then."

"That's not even the worst of it. She asked me to go get the man."

"What?' He took his eyes off the road only long enough to glance at me in surprise.

"Oh, yes. When I explained that kidnapping someone from a nursing home is a felony, she settled for me going to visit him and bringing back pictures of any photographs he might have." I groaned. "What have I gotten myself into, Grandpa?"

"A mess, it sounds like." He drove in silence for a minute before saying, "I understand where Max is coming from. She's in the unenviable position of having no immediate family members left and only a few distant relatives. Plus, we're the only ones that we know of who can communicate with her."

"I know," I said. "And I sympathize with her wanting to get to know the relatives she does have. But the fact remains, she's dead."

He scratched his head. "I feel like she loses sight of that sometimes, especially since you've done so much to make her feel alive. Look at what all she's able to do now: she reads, she watches movies and television programs, she listens to music, and now she can even reach out to other people through social media."

"And I'm glad of all those things." I sighed. "And I know Max is smart enough to consider the repercussions of her actions."

"You'll have to be patient with her, Pup. Want me to go with you to the nursing home?"

"Please. Maybe we can go Sunday after lunch? That is, if I can find out which one Dwight lives at."

"You will," he said. "I have no doubt about it."

When I got to the auditorium, Kristen was standing outside the door. And she was already mid-tantrum. My stomach rolled over as I considered why she might be fuming. If her anger was directed at me, I thought it had to be the dress. Somehow, it had been destroyed, and I was going to have to remake it.

"My life is ruined!" Kristen cried.

Feeling sicker by the second, I asked, "What's wrong? Did something happen to the dress?"

"The dress? No. It's my hair!"

I gave her head a cursory examination. Beautiful. Not a hair out of place. I squinted in confusion.

Exaggeratedly rolling her eyes at my obvious stupidity, Kristen said, "Mom won't let me get caramel highlights for the play. She says it's too close to the Miss Winter Garden High pageant and that the judges might not look favorably on color-treated hair."

"I—"

Ignoring that I was about to speak, Kristen paced and ranted. "It probably wouldn't even look color treated. Kim West gets her hair professionally colored, and you can't even tell. It looks fantastic. And you know what else? Kim is even allergic to hair dye!" She stopped at looked at me to see what I thought of that amazing revelation.

"Then how—?"

"How does she get it colored then? Her hairdresser mixes artificial sweetener—that saccharin stuff—into the dye, and it changes the PH level so Kim can tolerate the color." She made a growly sound. "Why does my mom have to be so freakin' uptight about everything? Ugh! She's ruining my life!"

I pulled out my phone and did a quick online search for clip-in caramel hair extensions. Turning my screen toward Kristen, I asked, "What about something like this?"

Grabbing my phone out of my hand, she frantically scrolled through the search results. As her scrolling slowed, she appeared to relax. "This would work. Could you help me put them in?"

"Sure." I steadied myself as Kristen threw her arms around me and gave me such a fierce hug that she nearly knocked me down.

After texting a link to herself, she returned my phone. "Thanks, Amanda." She hurried off to join the rest of the cast.

I was ironing the candlestick costume when I heard someone clear his throat. Glancing up, I saw Fergus Kramer striding toward me.

"Hello. We haven't met yet. I'm Fergus Kramer."

"It's nice to meet you, Mr. Kramer. I'm—"

"I know who you are, Ms. Tucker." He chuckled. "In fact, I had to come back here and meet the enchantress for myself."

Frowning slightly, I lifted the candlestick costume off the ironing board and hung it on a rack. "I'm hardly that."

"Don't sell yourself short." He wagged a finger at me. "Earlier this afternoon, Kristen Holbrook was in full-blown dramatic diva mode. I saw her speaking with you, and the next thing I knew, she was laughing and singing."

"I'm glad I could help." Here I was finally face to face with the man Blake Talbot was accusing of embezzlement to anyone who'd listen, and I had no idea what to say to him.

"Not only that, you've turned my wife into a movie star with the suit she bought from your boutique."

I laughed, feeling even more awkward that the man had sought me out to heap praise on me. What did he want? "I can't take credit for that, Mr. Kramer. Your wife is a lovely woman."

He beamed. "That she is. Well, you're obviously busy, so I won't keep you. But please let me know if there's anything you need while you're here at the school."

I couldn't let him go without trying to get him to talk about Sandra Kelly and Blake Talbot. "Wait." Once I'd made sure no one else was listening to our conversation, I said, "Actually, there is one thing."

"What's that?" he asked.

"Diana told me that you'd caught Sandra Kelly and Blake Talbot in the hall together when they were supposed to be teaching their respective classes." I spread my hands. "I heard the students gossiping about them the first evening I was here as well. What I'm wondering is why they weren't disciplined for their actions. I mean, there were two classrooms filled with neglected students who could attest to the fact that they were left unsupervised during class periods."

"It's my observation that students typically don't mind having their teachers out of the room," he said. "Also, Mr. Talbot hasn't liked me since I refused to approve a field trip for his golf team. His animosity toward me is well known here, and that's why I didn't report seeing him and Ms. Kelly together during their scheduled class time. I was afraid my accusation would be summarily dismissed."

"Still, you couldn't have been the only staff member to have noticed their behavior," I said. "I've only met Mr. Talbot once, and I didn't speak with Ms. Kelly but a couple of times, so I'm not acquainted with either of them. But if they'd had something that required that much discussion, they should have been conversing after school hours. Isn't there something Dr. Holbrook could've done?"

"I'm not sure if Maria was even aware of the situation."

I didn't contradict him, but I knew that wasn't true. Dr. Holbrook had told me herself last night that she absolutely knew and had been about to see if she could get both teachers fired.

"I'm sorry." I shook my head slightly. "She mentioned to me yesterday evening that you and she have been friends for years. I thought you might've brought the matter to her attention."

"It wasn't my place." He tapped his fingertips together. "As I'm sure you're well aware, being branded a troublemaker is always bad for business."

"Right." Had he just threatened me? Or was he warning me to mind my own business?

"Again, give me a holler if you should need anything," he said, as he left the auditorium.

Chapter Twenty-Eight

When Zoe came backstage a short while later, she found me staring off into space. "Hey. You all right?"

I nodded. "It's been a rather aggravating day. Nothing a good night's sleep can't fix. I hope."

"Wanna talk about it?"

If I ever wanted to gain Zoe's trust, I should probably confide in her first. "Well, I have a good friend who's flaking out on me. She..." How could I explain that Max can't go anywhere? "She has mobility issues but wanted to meet a guy she met online."

"And you're afraid he's a creep?" she asked.

"No, he's more than likely a nice man, but I can't simply go get him like she wants me to—he's in a nursing home."

She laughed. "Your friend sounds like a riot."

"She is. But I'm not willing to kidnap a guy from a nursing home for her."

Zoe gave into another fit of giggles, and this time I joined in.

"My Papaw is in a nursing home, and we have to get all kinds of special permission if we want to take him home for Thanksgiving or something," she said.

"See? But Max couldn't care less. Go get him, she says."

"Max? She's the friend you live-streamed the halftime show for, right?"

"Yep. Good memory." I blew out a breath. "That wasn't my only weird experience of the day though. Do you know Mr. Kramer?"

"I know who he is. Why? What did he do?"

I told her about him coming to meet me. "He was very complimentary, and I wondered why. I guess I'm a cynic. But, does he do that a lot? Flatter people, I mean."

She shrugged. "I haven't heard anyone talking about it if he does. But I've found that, typically, anybody blowing smoke up your butt either wants something from you or is getting ready to stab you in the back. I'd be careful if I were you."

Gee, she was awfully young to have such a jaded outlook. I didn't know whether to feel bad for her or glad that her maturity was likely to keep her safe. "I will."

"Oh, hey, my mom said it's all right for me to come work with you on Saturdays and that if you'll pick me up, she can come get me after work."

"Great. I'm happy we'll be working together."

"Me too. We can use the extra money." She wrinkled her forehead. "Back to Mr. Kramer, do be careful like I said, but don't worry about him too awful much. Kristen Holbrook thinks you're awesome, and her parents practically run this place. She'll make sure you're taken care of."

"Zoe, I need to tell you something, and I hope you won't be angry with me," I said gently. "I saw in Sandra Kelly's planner that she'd made a note to call Child Protective Services about you."

She nodded. "They came and went. Mom was furious with Ms. Kelly for interfering, but CPS didn't find anything wrong. Just because we don't live like the Holbrooks doesn't mean their lives are better. Right?"

"Absolutely." I paused. "I'm not so sure the Holbrooks' lives are as enviable as we might think either."

As I worked on the wardrobe costume, I decided I needed to know what Sandra Kelly and Fergus Kramer had argued about on the first evening Grandpa and I came here to Winter Garden High. She'd berated the man in front of several people, so someone would surely know. Since Dr. Holbrook and Mr. Kramer were such good friends, I thought maybe Kristen would know.

I got the opportunity to talk with Kristen later on while I was waiting for Grandpa to join me in the parking lot.

"See you, Amanda!" she called to me. "Thanks again for suggesting the extensions."

"You're welcome. Do you have a second before you leave?"

"Yeah," she said, as she walked over to me. "What's up?"

"Mr. Kramer came to say hello earlier this evening. He went out of his way to be nice to me, and I couldn't help but wonder what he and Ms. Kelly were fussing about the first evening I was here."

"Oh, I remember that. He was mad because Ms. Kelly wanted to be in charge of the finances for the play," Kristen said. "She told him she was in charge of the production and wanted to oversee every aspect of it. And he accused her of not trusting him. She said that had nothing to do with it."

"Do you believe it did?" I asked.

"I don't know. Ms. Kelly was nice, but she was a control freak, and Mr. Kramer has always been a mealy-mouthed little man. It could've been that Ms. Kelly was just trying to push him around." She smiled. "Apparently, she didn't realize my mom was involved. Ms. Kelly might've succeeded in dragging Mr. Kramer around by the nose, but nobody pushes Dr. Maria Holbrook around. Nobody."

That night, I had a dream. Someone was smoking a cigarette and touched it to Sandra Kelly's hair. The poor woman's entire head went up in flames. As I stood there gaping at Sandra, the person—who was nothing more than a shadowy figure—held the cigarette out toward me. The message was clear. I was next.

As you might imagine, I was shaken up by that nightmare. That's why I left Jazzy at home on Friday morning and went straight to Indulgences Beauty Salon. Someone there had answers about Sandra's death. I was sure of it.

There was a skinny, pink-haired girl standing against the building vaping when I walked up. The smoke smelled like pina colada.

"Hi," I said. "Do you work here?"

"Yes. What do you need?" She appraised my appearance. "Some light blue streaks would look awesome in your hair."

"Thanks, but I'm wondering who did Sandra Kelly's hair last Thursday. She was supposed to see Karen, but Karen was out sick."

Pinkie shrugged. "I don't know, hon. I don't work on Thursdays. All I know is that when I came in Friday morning, my vape juice bottle was on the floor, and it was empty. I pitched a fit. I can understand someone knocking it off accidentally, but whoever did it needed to pay for it."

"I agree. People can be so inconsiderate."

"You're telling me," she said.

"Thanks for your help." I turned to get back into my car.

"If you change your mind about those streaks, come one back. Ask for Jessica."

I promised I would. Then I got into my car and drove to the police station.

"I need to see Detective Cranston," I told the desk clerk.

The detective had overheard me and came out of his office. "Come on back, Ms. Tucker."

He said it with the resigned air of someone patronizing a pest, but I didn't care.

I followed Detective Cranston to his office and sat on the chair in front of his desk. "I won't take up but a minute of your time, but there's something I feel you should know."

Sitting down behind the desk, he said, "Shoot."

"This morning, I went back to Indulgences Beauty Salon to—"

"Ms. Tucker, please stop doing my job for me. I'm more than capable of—"

"Hear me out." I could interrupt as well as he could. Maybe better.

He flipped his palms. "Go ahead."

"Thank you. I went back there this morning and there was a pink-haired girl standing outside vaping. Now, she didn't work on Thursday, but she said when she came back in on Friday, her bottle of vape juice was empty." I carefully watched his expression. It didn't change. Did that mean he knew this already? "The person who killed Sandra Kelly was the stylist who colored her hair that afternoon."

"Are you finished, Ms. Tucker?" He stood.

"Yes." I stood and moved toward the door, feeling sorry I'd wasted my time.

"Ms. Tucker?"

I turned back to face him.

"I do appreciate your time and your diligence," he said. "But police work is dangerous and should be left to the professionals."

Chapter Twenty-Nine

When I got to work, I learned that I'd caused a small-scale panic there. Could I not do anything right today? Connie, Frank, and Ella said they were worried when I wasn't there at my usual time.

Connie immediately noticed I didn't have the cat carrier and asked, "Where's Jasmine? Did something happen to her?"

I assured everyone that I was fine and so was Jazzy. "I simply had an errand I had to take care of this morning." I was truly grateful for everyone's care and concern, but I wasn't that late.

And then I unlocked the door to the atelier and had to face the wrath of Max.

"Where in blazes have you been? You're more than an hour late! I have been walking the floors worried sick about you."

"Slow down, Mom," I said softly. "Everything is fine."

"Everything is not fine, and oh, good grief, I do sound like Mother. What a disaster." She stopped raving and laughed. "Well, shucks. The next time you're gonna be late, let me know, would you?"

"I'll do my best."

"So, where've you been anyway?" she asked.

I told her about going to the salon and then to Detective Cranston's office. "I know they're already looking into the salon—or, at least, I hope they are, but I know that whoever killed Sandra was the person who did her hair that night." I frowned. "And I'm worried it was Diana."

"I'm afraid you might be right. But don't jump to conclusions. Just because her husband was stealing from the school, and Sandra Kelly was trying to pinch him for it..." Her eyes widened. "Oh, Diana definitely bumped off Sandra Kelly."

Before we could discuss it further, Frank came into the atelier with a metal contraption. "Good morning. I'm ready to work on the ottoman if you are." He held up the apparatus so that I could see it was the bustle-type thing we'd discussed.

I grinned. "I think this is exactly what we need to do this morning."

Frank and I worked on the ottoman until after lunch. It wasn't until after we'd finished that Frank ate the lunch Ella had packed him that morning. He offered to share, but I told him I'd brought something. I had—a granola bar. Besides, I was getting down to the wire on these costumes, and I didn't have time to waste more time than I already had today. Going by Indulgences and the police station had eaten up too much of my day.

Once Frank and I completed the ottoman costume, I finished the wardrobe and then started on the teacup. Joey Conrad would be at the school tonight, and I wanted to get his costume done so I could be certain it wasn't too long.

By the time I looked up at the clock, it was nearly closing time. I called Grandpa and asked him to go on to the school without me.

"I'll be there," I promised. "I'm running a little late is all, trying to get Joey's costume finished."

It was dark when I pulled into the parking lot, so I took a space near a streetlight. A car drove into the lot behind me. I paid little attention to it, knowing there were other parents and volunteers coming and going. Especially with the middle school students in attendance tonight, there would be a lot of traffic.

Getting out of my car, I heard someone call my name. I looked around to see Diana Kramer.

Trying to hide the prickle of fear I felt, I called, "Hi, Diana!"

"We need to talk," she said, approaching my car.

"All right," I said. "Let's go inside here and talk in the auditorium."

"No. We need to talk here." She was almost face to face with me now. "I know you've been asking a lot of questions at the salon."

"I have. I..." I struggled with what to say. "I think someone there might've spoken to Sandra Kelly before she died. They might know what frame of mind she was in or if she said anything that would lead to finding her killer."

"Why is that any of your business?" she asked.

"The woman worked alongside your husband. I'd think you'd be concerned about who killed her too."

"I'm not. No one else has anything to fear." She brought a pistol out from behind her back. "Except maybe you."

"You should turn yourself in, Diana," I said. "Detective Cranston knows everything." Did he? Maybe.

Anyway, it sounded good...like he could be on his way right this minute to arrest Diana. "Why would you go to such lengths to cover up your husband's theft? Was it really that big a deal?"

"I never meant to kill Sandra Kelly," she hissed. "I only meant to make her sick and scare her a little. She was so high and mighty when she came into Indulgences and told me she knew Fergus was stealing. Well, you know what? Fergus didn't steal a thing. It was me."

"You?" My eyes darted from side to side, looking for a way out of this precarious position.

"Yes, me. I'd take a little money here and there from Fergus's petty cash box and leave a receipt to explain the missing funds." She tilted her head slightly. "That was easy enough, and since I'd been forging his signature for years on various documents, I found that writing a check on the school's account wasn't that hard either."

"What did Fergus say when he noticed the discrepancies?" I asked.

"Nothing. He didn't find out. I was careful and never took too much at once. Fergus...well, he took his job with a grain of salt and never looked too closely at the books," she said. "And then Sandra Kelly came around making accusations—she was going to ruin my marriage just like she'd destroyed her own."

"Were you two arguing at the salon? I mean, why would she stay in your chair if she knew you were angry with her?" My hand went involuntarily to my hair. "I'd be afraid you'd cut some of my hair off out of spite if you were angry at me."

She snickered. "Don't think I wasn't tempted. But then I saw Jessica's vape juice. And, anyway, Sandra and I weren't arguing. I was sweet as pie, asking Sandra to please let me talk to Fergus before she did. I told her there had to be a reasonable explanation for everything. I had her feeling sorry for me—the blindly devoted wife."

"If Sandra's death was an accident, Diana, then surely the police will take that into consideration. You need to tell them your side of the story."

"Good try," she said, "but I can't let you ruin my life any more than I could let Sandra. I really wish you'd have just left well enough alone." She raised the gun.

Widening my eyes, I looked over her shoulder and said, "Detective Cranston!"

When Diana glanced to the side, I grabbed the arm with the gun. She wasn't very big, and I was able to keep her arm pointed up in the air. It was a struggle though, until someone came up behind Diana and pulled her other arm up behind her back.

"Keep moving, and I'll break your arm."

Diana stopped fighting, and I did too, anxious to see who'd come to my aid. It was Maggie Flannagan.

"I've called 911," she said. "The police are on their way."

As if on cue, I heard sirens in the distance.

Within minutes, the police had Diana Kramer handcuffed and in the back of a squad car. Everyone who'd been inside the school had come outside to witness all the excitement. And, after reassuring Grandpa I was fine, I went in search of Maggie Flannagan.

She was standing near her car with Zoe.

"Hey," I said. "Thank you for saving my life."

"Ah, you had her," Maggie said. "Thanks for giving my kid a job."

Quoting Casablanca, Zoe looked from her mom to me. "Louis, I think this is the beginning of a beautiful friendship."

Saturday morning as I drove to pick up Zoe, I felt as if I had sawdust in my eyes. I hadn't had much sleep the night before. Between Grandpa fussing over me, my going online to fill Max in on the situation, and getting a call from Jason after he'd heard about the altercation in the parking lot, I hadn't gotten into bed until late. And then I'd lain awake thinking about Diana Kramer, her husband, and Sandra Kelly.

I pulled up to Zoe's modest home, and Maggie waved to me from the door. I waved back. Moments later, Zoe came barreling out the door.

"Last night was crazy." Seeing Jazzy's carrier on the backseat as she got into the car, she said, "Hi, Cat. What's her name again?"

"Jasmine, but I call her Jazzy most of the time."

"Cool." She buckled her seatbelt and waved good-bye to her mom.

During our conversation last night, I'd reminded Max that I was bringing Zoe to work this morning, and I'd warned her that I wouldn't be able to talk with her until after Zoe left. She'd said she was all right with that, but I knew she'd pop in to observe.

I was right.

When we walked into Designs on You, Max was sitting on the worktable swinging her legs. "Hello, darling."

"Hi. I'm Zoe. Who're you?"

My jaw dropped. "Who—? Who are you talking to?"

"The flapper lady who spoke to us when we came in." Zoe frowned at me. "Are you feeling all right?"

"Um...I'm fine. I'm surprised you can see Max, that's all."

"Oh, you're Max? I've heard a lot about you." Cocking her head, she said, "You don't look like you have a mobility problem though."

"Well, it isn't so much a mobility problem..." I trailed off, not quite knowing how to finish that sentence.

"I'm tethered to this building," Max explained. "Have you always had a gift for seeing ghosts?"

Zoe's eyes shifted from Max to me—twice. Then she slowly grinned. "You two are pranking me! I wondered about Max's crazy getup."

I gently ushered her into a chair. "We aren't kidding. Most people can't see or hear Max. To our knowledge, only Grandpa Dave and I can—and now you."

"You're—"

Connie's rapid-fire knock rattled the door.

I put my finger to my lips to instruct Zoe to be quiet. "Just watch."

"Hi," Connie said, as she stepped into the room and gave me a brief hug. "I didn't get a chance to see you last night during all the excitement. I'm so happy you're okay. Diana Kramer..." She shook her head. "Who'd have ever thought?" She turned to Zoe. "Oh, hi. I don't think we've officially met, but I'm Connie. I own Delightful Home. I'm right across the hall if you need anything."

As Connie spoke, Max went over to her and waved a hand in front of her face. Nothing. She poked her tongue out. No response from Connie. Finally, Max began singing some nonsense song to her. Connie completely ignored her.

"Connie, this is Zoe," I said. "She's going to be helping me out here on Saturdays."

"It's so nice to meet you, Zoe. I've seen you around the school, and I look forward to getting to know you."

"Likewise," Zoe said.

"Well, I'd better get back at it," Connie said. "I simply wanted to say hello and that I'm glad you're okay. See you later."

After Connie left, Zoe deflated slightly into the chair. "I don't understand."

"I don't either." Max stooped down in front of her. "But I'm so happy! I just found out day before yesterday that I have living relatives. Maybe somehow we're related."

That's it. "Zoe, what's your papaw's name?" I asked.

"Dwight Hall."

Max squealed with excitement. "You're my—"

I could nearly see the wheels spinning in Max's brain. "Great, great niece."

"Yes! That!" She squealed again. "I'm your Aunt Max!"

Although she still hadn't quite recovered from seeing a ghost, Zoe shook her head slightly. "Then you're the reason my name is Zoe Maxine. Our family has had a Maxine in it since my great-grandmother named my grandpa's sister that."

"Your great-grandmother was my sister." Max's eyes filled with tears.

Zoe looked over at me. "Doesn't the fact that she's a ghost creep you out?"

I shrugged. "You'll get used to it."

Epilogue

Beauty and the Beast opened to a packed house that included Frank, Ella, Grandpa, Ford, Connie's family, and Maggie Flannagan. Thanks to an in with the stage manager, Maxine Englebright was watching through live streaming on social media from my phone, which was set up on a tripod at the corner of the stage.

The play began with the witch turning the prince into a beast. Shortly thereafter, lovely Kristen with her caramel hair extensions strolled out onto the stage reading a book. Her parents both looked so proud they could burst.

As Kristen/Belle walked through the village, Connie teared up at seeing Marielle singing and dancing while carrying a basket filled with flowers among the rest of the villagers. Frank puffed out his chest nearly half an hour into the play when the enchanted furniture—including the ottoman—cavorted around the castle. I have to admit, I was feeling a little pleased with myself at that point too.

Sarah Conrad and her husband sat behind me, and she squeezed my shoulder when Joey made his first appearance as Chip. I turned slightly to wink at her and saw that Biscuit and Gravy were safely in a small blue carrier on Sarah's lap.

Grandpa and Ford elbowed each other and smiled smugly as Gaston fell from their well-crafted balcony onto the stack of yoga mats from the gym. The men were certain that, to the audience, it appeared the young man had fallen for at least a hundred feet.

After the play, Connie and I hosted a staff party of sorts at Shops on Main. Although it wasn't the open house I'd been longing to have, it was great fun. Max traipsed around all the guests, mingling and talking as if they could hear every witty word she said. And three of us could.

The next morning, the play and the party was all Max could talk about. She gushed over it, rehashing scene after scene, until Zoe called us on social media.

"Hi," I said, as I accepted her video chat request.

"Is Max there?" she asked.

"Right here." Max came to sit beside me. "You did a wonderful job with the play last night. It was amazing! And wasn't the party the most fun ever?"

"There's someone here who wants to meet you." She moved her phone slightly, and an older man's face filled the screen. "How many people do you see, Papaw?"

Max gasped.

"I see two pretty young ladies," he said. "And one of them reminds me of my mother."

"Hi, Mr. Hall," I said.

"Hello," he said. "How are you?"

Reaching out, Max's hand went through the screen.

"We're fine," I said.

"Dwight," Max said at last.

"That's right. What's your name?" he asked.

"I'm Maxine."

He laughed. "That was my sister's name. Maxines are feisty. We always make sure to have one in our family."

"That's right," Zoe said. She held up a photograph of Dot. "Look, Max. Recognize this young lady?"

Max nodded, tears streaming down her cheeks.

"I'm making you a copy of it, and I'll give it to Amanda at the play tonight." Zoe moved the photo away and put the focus on Dwight again. "I think you and Aunt Max will have some catching up to do one of these days, but for now, I believe you both should rest a while. See you soon."

"See you, darling." Max wiped her eyes before turning to me. "This social media stuff is the elephant's eyebrows!"

Gayle Leeson is a pseudonym for Gayle Trent, an author living in Virginia with a beautiful family and quite a few pets. I also write as Amanda Lee. As Gayle Trent, I write the Daphne Martin Cake Mystery series and the Myrtle Crumb Mystery series. As Amanda Lee, I write the Embroidery Mystery series. As Gayle Leeson, I write the Down South Cafe mystery series, the Ghostly Fashionista mystery series, and the Kinsey Falls women's fiction series.

Please visit me online at http://www.gayleleeson.com and http://www.ghostlyfashionista.com.

In case you missed it, take a look at Book One in the Ghostly Fashionista mystery series:

DESIGNS ON MURDER

Chapter One

A   flash of brilliant light burst from the lower righthand window of Shops on Main, drawing my attention to the For Lease sign. I'd always loved the building and couldn't resist going inside to see the space available.

I opened the front door to the charming old mansion, which had started life as a private home in the late 1800s and had had many incarnations since then. I turned right to open another door to go into the vacant office.

"Why so glum, chum?" asked a tall, attractive woman with a dark brown bob and an impish grin. She stood near the window wearing a rather fancy mauve gown for the middle of the day. She was also wearing a headband with a peacock feather, making her look like a flapper from the 1920s. I wondered if she might be going to some sort of party after work. Either that, or this woman was quite the eccentric.

"I just came from a job interview," I said.

"Ah. Don't think it went well, huh?"

"Actually, I think it did. But I'm not sure I want to be doing that kind of work for...well...forever."

"Nothing's forever, darling. But you've come to the right place. My name's Max, by the way. Maxine, actually, but I hate that stuffy old name. Maxine Englebright. Isn't that a mouthful? You can see why I prefer Max."

I chuckled. "It's nice to meet you, Max. I'm Amanda Tucker."

"So, Amanda Tucker," Max said, moving over to the middle of the room, "what's your dream job?"

"I know it'll sound stupid. I shouldn't have even wandered in here--"

"Stop that please. Negativity gets us nowhere."

Max sounded like a school teacher then, and I tried to assess her age. Although she somehow seemed older, she didn't look much more than my twenty-four years. I'd put her at about thirty...if that. Since she was looking at me expectantly, I tried to give a better answer to her question.

"I want to fill a niche...to make some sort of difference," I said. "I want to do something fun, exciting...something I'd look forward to doing every day."

"And you're considering starting your own business?"

"That was my initial thought upon seeing that this space is for lease. I love this building...always have."

"What sort of business are you thinking you'd like to put here?" Max asked.

"I enjoy fashion design, but my parents discouraged me because—they said—it was as hard to break into as professional sports. I told them there are a lot of people in professional sports, but they said, 'Only the best, Mandy.'"

Max gave an indignant little bark. "Oh, that's hooey! But I can identify. My folks never thought I'd amount to much. Come to think of it, I guess I didn't." She threw back her head and laughed.

"Oh, well, I wish I could see some of your designs."

"You can. I have a couple of my latest right here on my phone." I took my cell phone from my purse and pulled up the two designs I'd photographed the day before. The first dress had a small pink and green floral print on a navy background, shawl collar, three-quarter length sleeves, and A-line skirt. "I love vintage styles."

"This is gorgeous! I'd love to have a dress like this."

"Really?"

"Yeah. What else ya got?" Max asked.

My other design was an emerald 1930s-style bias cut evening gown with a plunging halter neckline and a back panel with pearl buttons that began at the middle of the back on each side and went to the waist.

Max caught her breath. "That's the berries, kid!"

"Thanks." I could feel the color rising in my cheeks. Max might throw out some odd phrases, but I could tell she liked the dress. "Mom and Dad are probably right, though. Despite the fact that I use modern fabrics—some with quirky, unusual patterns—how could I be sure I'd have the clientele to actually support a business?"

"Are you kidding me? People would love to have their very own fashion designer here in little ol' Abingdon."

"You really think so? Is it the kind of place you'd visit?" I asked.

"Visit?" Max laughed. "Darling, I'd practically live in it."

"All right. I'll think about it."

"Think quickly please. There was someone in here earlier today looking at the space. He wants to sell cigars and tobacco products. Pew. The smell would drive me screwy. I'd much rather have you here."

Hmm...the lady had her sales pitch down. I had to give her that. "How much is the rent?"

"Oh, I have no idea. You'll find Mrs. Meacham at the top of the stairs, last door on your left. It's marked OFFICE."

"Okay. I'll go up and talk with her."

"Good luck, buttercup!"

I was smiling and shaking my head as I mounted the stairs. Max was a character. I thought she'd be a fun person to have around.

Since the office wasn't a retail space like the other rooms in the building, I knocked and waited for a response before entering.

Mrs. Meacham was a plump, prim woman with short, curly white hair and sharp blue eyes. She looked at me over the top of her reading glasses. "How may I help you?"

"I'm interested in the space for rent downstairs," I said.

"You are? Oh, my! I thought you were here selling cookies or something. You look so young." Mrs.

Meacham laughed at her own joke, so I faked a chortle to be polite. "What type of shop are you considering?"

"A fashion boutique."

"Fashion?"

"Yes, I design and create retro-style fashions."

"Hmm. I never picked up sewing myself. I've never been big on crafts." She stood and opened a file cabinet to the left of her desk, and I could see she was wearing a navy suit. "Canning and baking were more my strengths. I suppose you could say I prefer the kitchen to the hearth." She laughed again, and I chuckled along with her.

She turned and handed me an application. "Just read this over and call me back if you have any questions. If you're interested in the space, please let me know as soon as possible. There's a gentleman interested in opening a cigar store there." She tapped a pen on her desk blotter. "But even if he gets here before you do, we'll have another opening by the first of the month. The web designer across the hall is leaving. Would you like to take a look at his place before you decide?"

"No, I'd really prefer the shop on the ground floor," I said.

"All right. Well, I hope to hear from you soon."

I left then. I stopped back by the space for lease to say goodbye to Max, but she was gone.

I went home--my parents' home actually, but they moved to Florida for Dad's job more than two years ago, so it was basically mine...until they wanted it back. I made popcorn for lunch, read over Mrs. Meacham's contract, and started crunching the numbers.

I'd graduated in May with a bachelor's degree in business administration with a concentration in marketing and entrepreneurship but just couldn't find a position that sparked any sort of passion in me. This morning I'd had yet another interview where I'd been overqualified for the position but felt I had a good chance of getting an offer...a low offer...for work I couldn't see myself investing decades doing.

Jasmine, my cat, wandered into the room. She'd eaten some kibble from her bowl in the kitchen and was now interested in what I was having. She hopped onto the coffee table, peeped into the popcorn bowl, and turned away dismissively to clean her paws. She was a beautiful gray and white striped tabby. Her feet were white, and she looked as if she were wearing socks of varying lengths--crew socks on the back, anklets on the front.

"What do you think, Jazzy?" I asked. "Should I open a fashion boutique?"

She looked over her shoulder at me for a second before resuming her paw-licking. I didn't know if that was a yes or a no.

Even though I'd gone to school for four years to learn all about how to open, manage, and provide inventory for a small business, I researched for the remainder of the afternoon. I checked out the stats on independent designers in the United States and fashion boutiques in Virginia. There weren't many in the Southwest Virginia region, so I knew I'd have something unique to offer my clientele.

Finally, Jazzy let me know that she'd been napping long enough and that we needed to do something. Mainly, I needed to feed her again, and she wanted to eat. But I had other ideas.

"Jazzy, let's get your carrier. You and I are going to see Grandpa Dave."

Grandpa Dave was my favorite person on the planet, and Jazzy thought pretty highly of him herself. He lived only about ten minutes away from us. He was farther out in the country and had a bigger home than we did. Jazzy and I were happy in our little three-bedroom, one bath ranch. We secretly hoped Dad wouldn't lose the job that had taken him and Mom to Florida and that they'd love it too much to leave when he retired because we'd gotten used to having the extra space.

I put the carrier on the backseat of my green sedan. It was a cute car that I'd worked the summer between high school and college to get enough money to make the down payment on, but it felt kinda ironic to be driving a cat around in a car that reminded people of a hamster cage.

Sometimes, I wished my Mom and Dad's house was a bit farther from town. It was so peaceful out here in the country. Fences, pasture land, and cows bordered each side of the road. There were a few houses here and there, but most of the land was still farmland. The farmhouses were back off the road and closer to the barns.

When we pulled into Grandpa Dave's long driveway, Jazzy meowed.

"Yes," I told her. "We're here."

Grandpa Dave lived about fifty yards off the road, and his property was fenced, but he didn't keep any animals. He'd turned the barn that had been on the land when he and Grandma Jodie bought it into a workshop where he liked to "piddle."

I pulled around to the side of the house and was happy to see that, rather than piddling in the workshop, Grandpa was sitting on one of the white rocking chairs on the porch. I parked and got out, opened the door to both the car and the carrier for Jazzy, and she ran straight to hop onto his lap.

"Well, there's my girls!" Grandpa Dave laughed.

It seemed to me that Grandpa was almost always laughing. He'd lost a little of that laughter after Grandma Jodie had died. But that was five years ago, and, except for some moments of misty remembrance, he was back to his old self.

I gave him a hug and a kiss on the cheek before settling onto the swing.

"I was sorta expecting you today," he said. "How'd the interview go?"

"It went fine, I guess, but I'm not sure Integrated Manufacturing Technologies is for me. The boss was nice, and the offices are beautiful, but...I don't know."

"What ain't she telling me, Jazzy?"

The cat looked up at him adoringly before butting her head against his chin.

"I'm...um...I'm thinking about starting my own business." I didn't venture a glance at Grandpa Dave right away. I wasn't sure I wanted to know what he was thinking. I figured he was thinking I'd come to ask for money--which I had, money and advice—but I was emphatic it was going to be a loan.

Grandpa had already insisted on paying my college tuition and wouldn't hear of my paying him back. This time, I was giving him no choice in the matter. Either he'd lend me the money, and sign the loan agreement I'd drafted, or I wouldn't take it.

I finally raised my eyes to look at his face, and he was looking pensive.

"Tell me what brought this on," he said.

I told him about wandering into Shops on Main after my interview and meeting Maxine Englebright. "She loved the designs I showed her and seemed to think I could do well if I opened a boutique there. I went upstairs and got an application from the building manager, and then I went home and did some research. I'd never seriously considered opening my own business before--at least, not at this stage of my career--but I'd like to try."

Another glance at Grandpa Dave told me he was still listening but might take more convincing.

"I realize I'm young, and I'm aware that more than half of all small businesses fail in the first four years. But I've got a degree that says I'm qualified to manage a business. Why not manage my own?"

He remained quiet.

"I know that opening a fashion boutique might seem frivolous, but there aren't a lot of designers in this region. I believe I could fill a need...or at least a niche."

Grandpa sat Jazzy onto the porch and stood. Without a word, he went into the house.

Jazzy looked up at me. Meow? She went over to the door to see where Grandpa Dave went. Meow? She stood on her hind legs and peered through the door.

"Watch out, Jasmine," he said, waiting for her to hop down and back away before he opened the door. He was carrying his checkbook. "How much do you need?"

"Well, I have some savings, and--"

"That's not what I asked."

"Okay. Now, this will be a loan, Grandpa Dave, not a gift."

"If you don't tell me how much, I'm taking this checkbook back into the house, and we won't discuss it any further."

"Ten thousand dollars," I blurted.

As he was writing the check, he asked, "Have you and Jazzy had your dinner yet?"

We were such frequent guests that he kept her favorite cat food on hand.

"We haven't. Do you have the ingredients to make a pizza?"

He scoffed. "Like I'm ever without pizza-makings." He handed me the check. "By the way, how old is this Max you met today? She sounds like quite a gal."

"She doesn't look all that much older than me. But she seems more worldly...or something. I think you'd like her," I said. "But wait, aren't you still seeing Betsy?"

He shrugged. "Betsy is all right to take to Bingo...but this Max sounds like she could be someone special."

First thing the next morning, I went to the bank to set up a business account for Designs on You.

That's what I decided to name my shop. Then I went to Shops on Main and gave Mrs. Meacham my application. After she made sure everything was in order, she took my check for the first month's rent and then took me around to meet the rest of the shop owners.

She introduced me to the upstairs tenants first. There was Janice, who owned Janice's Jewelry. She was of average height but she wore stilettos, had tawny hair with blonde highlights, wore a shirt that was way too tight, and was a big fan of dermal fillers, given her expressionless face.

"Janice, I'd like you to meet Amanda," said Mrs. Meacham. "She's going to be opening a fashion boutique downstairs."

"Fashion? You and I should talk, Amanda. You dress them, and I'll accessorize them." She giggled before turning to pick up a pendant with a large, light green stone. "With your coloring, you'd look lovely in one of these Amazonite necklace and earring sets."

"I'll have to check them out later," I said. "It was nice meeting you."

Janice grabbed a stack of her business cards and pressed them into my hand. "Here. For your clients. I'll be glad to return the favor."

"Great. Thanks."

Next, Mrs. Meacham took me to meet Mark, a web site designer. Everything about Mark screamed thin. The young man didn't appear to have an ounce of fat on his body. He had thinning black hair. He wore a thin crocheted tie. He held out a thin hand for me to shake. His handshake was surprisingly firm.

"Hello. It's a pleasure to meet you, Amanda." He handed me a card from the holder on his desk. "Should you need any web design help or marketing expertise, please call on me. I can work on a flat fee or monthly fee basis, depending on your needs."

"Thank you, but--"

"Are you aware that fifty percent of fledgling businesses fail within the first year?" he asked.

I started to correct his stats, but I didn't want to alienate someone I was going to be working near. I thanked him again and told him I appreciated his offer. It dawned on me as Mrs. Meacham and I were moving on to the next tenant that she'd said the web designer was leaving at the end of the month...which was only a week away. I wondered where he was taking his business.

The other upstairs shop was a bookstore called Antiquated Editions. The owner was a burly, bearded man who'd have looked more at home in a motorcycle shop than selling rare books, but, hey, you can't judge a book by its cover, right?

I made a mental note to tell Grandpa Dave my little joke. As you've probably guessed, I didn't have a lot of friends. Not that I wasn't a friendly person. I had a lot of acquaintances. It was just hard for me to get close to people. I wasn't the type to tell my deepest, darkest secrets to someone I hadn't known...well, all my life.

The brawny book man's name was Ford. I'd have been truly delighted had it been Harley, but had you been expecting me to say his name was Fitzgerald or Melville, please see the aforementioned joke about books and covers. He was friendly and invited me to come around and look at his collection anytime. I promised I'd do so after I got settled in.

Then it was downstairs to meet the rest of the shop owners. The first shop on the left when you came in the door--the shop directly across the hall from mine--was Delightful Home. The proprietress was Connie, who preferred a hug over a handshake.

"Aren't you lovely?" Connie asked.

I did not say I doubt it, which was the first thought that popped into my brain, but I did thank her for the compliment. Connie was herself the embodiment of lovely. She had long, honey blonde hair that she wore in a single braid. Large silver hoops adorned her ears, and she had skinny silver bracelets stacked up each arm. She wore an embroidered red tunic that fell to her thighs, black leggings, and Birkenstocks. But the thing that made her truly lovely wasn't so much her looks but the way she appeared to boldly embrace life. I mean, the instant we met, she embraced me. Her shop smelled of cinnamon and something else...sage, maybe.

"Melba, that blue is definitely your color," Connie said. "By the way, did that sinus blend help you?"

"It did!" Mrs. Meacham turned to me. "Connie has the most wonderful products, not the least of which are her essential oils."

I could see that Connie had an assortment of candles, soaps, lotions, oils, and tea blends. I was curious to see what all she did have, but that would have to wait.

"I'm here to help you in any way I possibly can," said Connie, with a warm smile. "Anything you need, just let me know. We're neighbors now."

Mrs. Meacham took me to meet the last of my "neighbors," Mr. and Mrs. Peterman.

"Call us Ella and Frank," Ella insisted. She was petite with salt-and-pepper hair styled in a pixie cut.

Frank was average height, had a slight paunch, a bulbous nose, and bushy brown hair. He didn't say much.

Ella and Frank had a paper shop. They designed their own greeting cards and stationery, and they sold specialty and novelty items that would appeal to their clientele. For instance, they had socks with book patterns, quotes from famous books, and likenesses of authors.

After I'd met everyone, Mrs. Meacham handed me the keys to my shop and went upstairs. Although my shop wouldn't open until the first of September, she'd graciously given me this last week of August to get everything set up.

I unlocked my door and went inside. I was surprised to see Max standing by the window. I started to ask her how she'd got in, but then I saw that there was another door that led to the kitchen. I imagined my space had once been the family dining room. Anyway, it was apparent that the door between my space and the kitchen hallway had been left unlocked. I'd have to be careful to check that in the future.

But, for now, I didn't mind at all that Max was there. Or that it appeared she was wearing the same outfit she'd been wearing yesterday. Must have been some party!

"So, you leased the shop?" Max asked.

"I did!"

"Congratulations! I wish we could have champagne to celebrate."

I laughed. "Me too, but I'm driving."

Max joined in my laughter. "I'm so glad you're going to be here. I think we'll be great friends."

"I hope so." And I truly did. I immediately envisioned Max as my best friend--the two of us going to lunch together, talking about guys and clothes, shopping together. I reined myself in before I got too carried away.

I surveyed the room. The inside wall to my right had a fireplace. I recalled that all the rooms upstairs had them too. But this one had built-in floor-to-ceiling bookshelves on either side of the fireplace.

"Does this fireplace still work?" I asked Max.

"I imagine it would, but it isn't used anymore. The owners put central heat and air in eons ago."

"Just checking. I mean, I wasn't going to light fire to anything. I merely wanted to be sure it was safe to put flammables on these shelves." I could feel my face getting hot. "I'm sorry. That was a stupid thing to say. I'm just so excited--"

"And I'm excited for you. You have nothing to apologize for. How were you supposed to know whether or not the former tenant ever lit the fireplace?"

"You're really nice."

"And you're too hard on yourself. Must you be brilliant and well-spoken all the time?"

"Well...I'm certainly not, but I'd like to be."

"Tell me what you have in store for this place," she said.

I indicated the window. "I'd like to have a table flanked by chairs on either side here." I bit my lip. "Where's the best place around here to buy some reasonably priced furniture that would go with the overall atmosphere of the building?"

"I have no idea. You should ask Connie."

"Connie?" I was actually checking to make sure I'd heard Max correctly, but it so happened that I'd left the door open and Connie was walking by as I spoke.

"Yes?"

"Max was telling me that you might know of a good furniture place nearby," I said.

"Max?" Connie looked about the room. "Who's Max?"

I whirled around, thinking Max had somehow slipped out of the room. But, nope, there she stood...shaking her head...and putting a finger to her lips.

"Um...she was....she was just here. She was here yesterday too. I assumed she was a Shops on Main regular."

"I don't know her, but I'd love to meet her sometime. As for the furniture, I'd try the antique stores downtown for starters. You might fall in love with just the right piece or two there." She grinned. "I'd better get back to minding the store. Good luck with the furniture shopping!"

Connie pulled the door closed behind her as she left, and I was glad. I turned to Max.

"Gee, that was awkward," she said. "I was sure you knew."

"Knew?"

"That I'm a ghost."